FIRE DRIFTER 1: Meteor Shower

By Carol Bellhouse

Cover Design by Dawn Beck

Photography by Carol Bellhouse

Copyright 2013 Carol Bellhouse

Published by Zuni Canyon Institute

Some of this is true.

Most of it isn't.

You decide.

I am on fire, back tires unweighted, sliding sideways. I float on the smoke, playing the engine against itself, locking in. Everything responds to my touch, to my request. Drifting in the night, time does not hold me.

Carol Dellhom

1971

Chapter 1

"When I was born, the sky fell to earth in a meteor shower." My voice floats in the dark air of the empty Opera House.

I'm eighteen, rehearsing lines on the stage of a magnificent theater built in 1879.

I turn, deliberately, languidly, looking out across the expanse of vacant seats. I practice running my eyes from seat to seat, observing coolly the faces that are not there yet.

"It's not enough just to be born, you know. Not even in a meteor shower." I pause, gauging my timing, and look out over the dusty gilded chairs, the worn red velvet. It has been a long time since the glory days when Leadville was king of the silver boom.

"Since it ends in the blink of an eye, in one final exhale," I recite, knowing the script, marked and tattered from the process and thrown somewhere offstage, unnecessary.

Theater is more real than life has ever been for me. It was the alternative to the reality that was handed to me at birth.

"I choose not the reality. Give me something else," I screamed from the crib. "There's been a mistake! Don't leave me here!"

So the bed sheets went up as the curtain and siblings were conscripted to play the parts. The neighbor kids eventually wandered into the action, not feeling it but going along anyway.

"It's important," I emphasized dramatically, "that the lines be delivered with emotion, from the heart, to engage the audience, to lift the performance!"

When I couldn't get the cooperation and the level of dedication I deserved in backyard theater, I resorted to dolls and puppets to give the performances I required. "Cry," I commanded and Barbie flailed and gasped in response.

School plays took it to the next level. Teachers gratefully turned over their rowdy classrooms for me to transform into sword fights and avalanches and double murders. No daisy-and-toadstool productions for me.

Lo and behold, it kept getting better. I walked into a community theater audition for "The Crucible," and got the part of Betty Parris, a screaming hysteric who faints dead away. It was heaven-- could it get any better?

It could. Community theater was vibrant for years and I was accepted and praised. I lit up like the Fourth of July. I didn't have to deal with the rest of my life--I was always at play practice.

High school productions soon overlapped community theater and I was gone, gone, gone-- all the time. Forever absent from home and the deadly forces at work there.

It was my lifeline. I followed it, hand over hand, trying to find a place to be, a place to breathe. I found it, temporary and fleeting, on stage. I put my all into it, losing myself in my characters, dreaming my role.

We did children's plays—Maggie's Magic Teapot, The Dancing Donkey. There were musicals— Oliver and Oklahoma. And heavy dramas—All My Sons and Diary of Anne Frank.

The town turned out. I signed autographs on programs. There were cast parties and write-ups in the Herald Democrat.

Now I've reached the pinnacle of what is possible in a small town. For my graduation, I'm performing a play written for me: Meteor Shower.

Except for excelling in sports, it's as high as I can get.

I turned eighteen last week. I'm striking but not beautiful, willowy but not shapely, creative but not intellectual. My red curls forewarn my temper and I'm fast and strong--a necessity for my survival so far.

There will be a full dress rehearsal in three days, on Saturday afternoon. The show goes up Saturday night, following graduation in the morning.

Francie Wilbur and I rehearse, working out the final blocking. She is the author of this masterpiece, my graduation gift. It's not my story, but it is my story.

Her voice interrupts me from the back of the theater. I glance to the shadows, following the sound of her low voice. "Okay, watch how you make your transition here."

I can't see her but I know she's nodding. She's been my English and theater teacher for three years now and it's ending here--with one final exhale.

The play is her baby--ten minutes, strong dialogue, exquisite pacing and one actress--me. I will carry it. I will open the talent show with it.

I think about the exhale. When I say the word on stage, my eyes on the audience, breathing out as I form the word, they will. They will exhale. They can't help it.

It's the power of the delivery and the force of the word itself. It's like water--clear and suggestive-- and binding.

"Sure," I say, pausing, giving myself an extra beat to find my character again. The next part is silent and visual.

I reach up to trace invisible walls, boundaries that box me on stage, to show that I'm captive.

I hear Francie walking down the aisle so I wait. She guides herself by touching the backs of the ornate seats, partly because it's dark and the slanting floor a little uneven, and partly because she's been drinking.

I smelled it when she came in. Not too much. Just enough to get there while keeping her job and her standing in the community.

"You know what, Madelyn?" she asks, not waiting for my answer. "When you're up there Saturday night, wearing all black? With just the spot on you? Your face and hands will look ethereal."

At forty, she's buxom and grand. She carries her large-boned framed with heavy elegance. "And you're going to nail the opening lines."

I adore Francie. She's one of the few people on earth who believes in me. It has not been easy so far and everyone in town knows it.

Leadville is a tough place, and historically so, beckoning with dreams of gold and silver and delivering thin air, unrelenting wind and snow and majestic views that dwarf the soul. The result is a handful of bitter, crushed people overwhelmed by sheer scale. People who drink.

Francie knows I love the play and the way she has crafted the words and the silences. She believes I will be using it for my audition in the fall for the theater department at Colorado State University.

I allow her to believe it. She doesn't know. She doesn't need to know. Because I'm making other plans. I'm daring life.

Francie sighs and lowers herself into a front row seat. She glances up, taking in the ceiling paintings and the heavy draperies in the private boxes.

"Madelyn," she says, "Do you really think it's a good idea?"

I panic. How does she know? Can she read my mind? I feel a flush cross my face and slow my breathing to counteract the adrenalin charge.

"What?" I ask, tentatively.

She misses my blush because she's been drinking, because she's looking at the frescoes, because it's late and we're both tired.

She sighs. "We know that some of the acts are not going to show up."

Ah, she's talking about the talent show, not my mutiny. I was the one who talked her into the show. Its success or failure falls squarely on my head. I pull my hands off the invisible wall and lower myself cross-legged onto the dusty floor of the stage.

"We move on to whoever's next," I say reasonably.

"And that old light board probably won't take the power drain."

"It might blow with the band at the end but a complete power failure will be exciting. Talked about for years to come," I muse.

Francie nods slowly, breathing her way through her fatigue. "Yeah," she says, "Yeah. One more Leadville story."

Just one more of so many.

Chapter 2

I wrestle with the double doors under the vaulted and corniced windows of the Opera House. I've run through the monologue once more and Francie seems satisfied. She knows I won't embarrass her. And I'm sure she needs a drink.

She gave me a hug when she left, whispering, "You're going to knock them dead." I gave her a squeeze back. I watched her leave and set about turning off the lights.

One man, Horace Tabor, built the Opera House presiding over the main street as a monument to the riches that Leadville handed him through serendipity and hard work, presupposing the dramatic turn his life would take.

He took a lot of chances. I guess it's in the air at this altitude. Chance could be my middle name.

But then again, I don't have much to lose. He didn't either.

I pull hard to make the doors line up so I can lock them. I've had a key to the Opera House since the summer of my junior year. I worked as a tour guide for two years before I was deemed trustworthy enough to have my own access.

"Damn it," I curse at the aged and warped doors refusing to cooperate.

I wonder if these are the original doors but decide they can't possibly be. I've seen lots of pictures of the Opera House in its heyday, when it was attached to the Clarendon Hotel by an enclosed elevated walkway. Lofty and lauded in its prime, it has narrowly escaped the fate of the Clarendon Hotel which burned to the ground and was demolished long before I was born.

"Come on," I plead. "You can do this. I know you've got it in you. One more time."

My begging works. With a weary finality, the doors give up the fight and my key turns in the lock. I hear the deadbolt slide into place. A bare bulb dangles over the entry, a far cry from the 72 jets of brightly-burning gas lights that lit her up in 1879.

I stand for a minute on the sidewalk, looking at the stars. "Star light, star bright," I begin, but realize that it doesn't apply because there are a million stars overhead transforming the dark night.

We're closer to the stars here than just about any place on earth so they are bright and crisp and fill the night. The Milky Way looks like someone took a knife and slashed through the fabric of the sky.

"Never mind," I amend.

My key ring rests in my hand and I finger past the Opera House key until I reach my car key.

I make a wish anyway.

The car is parked at the curb. It's not really my car. It's my brother's car. Rusty bought her two years ago brand new in 1969, using the money he got from his Navy enlistment to make the down payment.

"You waited," I acknowledge. Not that the car has ever left or abandoned me but a little appreciation goes a long way. I know that.

When he reported for basic training, Rusty entrusted me with this beauty, a 1969 Camaro, cherry red, with a V-8 engine that can take all comers. It's all he and I really have.

Rusty has dark hair and warm brown eyes, a ready laugh behind his shyness. He's a sharp contrast to my wild Scottish coloring--the unruly red hair and eyes as blue as the Highland sky. I got the Scottish side of things, including the wild child in me that has always driven our parents to distraction. They much preferred Rusty's quiet, dark Druid-ness. I was too much trouble.

"There's a reason the English built Hadrian's Wall and it wasn't to keep the British in," I murmur to myself.

I slide my hand in a caress across the roof of the car, all shiny and slick, as I unlock the door.

"Your Highness, I am forever in your service." A lot of appreciation is even better. One can never take a '69 Camaro for granted. It goes without saying.

The engine kicks into a throbbing purr as I turn the key in the ignition. I ponder my options. Going home could not be further down the list. There's nothing but chaos and clutter there.

"No, not yet," I affirm to the car.

I could head out to Kristi Lanes, the bowling alley on the north end of town, to see who is hanging out there. On the south end of town, Dunn's Bar waits quietly on a side street off the highway, at the corner of Leiter and Elm. Since I turned eighteen, I can legally enter although I've been going there for years.

I don't like the smell of beer. Even 3.2 beer is a full reminder of everything that was wrong with my childhood. And beer has saturated the floorboards at Dunn's Bar for all the years the youth of Leadville have been learning to drink. It's an earthy smell, loamy and musky, embedded and permanent.

Jim Morrison is singing Don't You Love Her Madly on KOMA radio, winding eloquently through the Advent speakers Rusty installed in the Camaro on his last leave. The song mixes with the rumble of the exhaust pipes as I watch traffic go by on Harrison Avenue.

"Don't you love her as she's walking out the door?" asks Morrison, drowsy and hard.

I drop the Camaro into first gear and roll out on the avenue, turning left on Sixth Street through the green light. The Victorian houses stand mutely as I head out of the historic part of town, up the hill and out of town.

"We're doing the Loop," I tell the car, just so she knows. Driving the Loop always clears my head.

"Yeah, all your love is gone, so sing a lonely song..." laments Morrison as I settle the Camaro into third gear.

I consider stopping to pick up my friend, Bette, on the way but I already know this is a solo. I drive past Bette's house where Mama Rose holds court over five beautiful daughters in a locale where there's nothing but trouble. Bette's father is probably drunk at the Pioneer, talking to Ma Brown and waiting for one of his daughters to make the walk to Second Street to tell him that Rose wants him home.

"...Of a deep blue dream, seven horses seem to be on the mark," punctuates the song, the guitars taking over.

The pine trees slide past my windows. Leadville is so close to timberline that pines are the only tree tough enough to handle the altitude and the cold.

After a fire, aspen trees come in as secondary growth, taking hold and creating brilliant swaths of gold and red in the fall.

It's still too cold for aspens to be in leaf. It's the end of May, still snowing at night. They are thick in bud and not willing to commit until the temperatures climb above freezing.

It's been another long winter. I feel the anger rising in me. It always does. I know what to do. Rusty taught me.

Chapter 3

It's a Doors' set on KOMA as the road narrows and I come into the first turn.

"Riders on the storm," begins Morrison, lulling and hypnotic.

I drop my hand to the gear shift and take down the clutch, increasing my RPMs.

"Into this house we're born," chants the song, speaking to me.

I downshift to second gear and release the clutch. The power surge makes the back wheels lose traction and I slide through the first turn, wheels smoking.

"Into this world we're thrown," Morrison sings as I take the second turn at a higher speed, feeling the suspension pull the car down.

"Like a dog without a bone..."

The thrill of the power surge builds as I hit the third curve and straighten, relaxing on the gas pedal.

"An actor out on loan..."

It's a heady rush and my breathing has stepped up even though I've consciously kept my heart rate down and my grip on the wheel as light as I can without losing control.

"Riders on the storm..."

I've come through the three curves perfectly. Rusty would be proud. I check my rearview mirror to make sure no cars are behind me, specifically a police car, and smile. I'm clear.

"There you have it, Rusty boy." He came out of Vietnam on the last tour unscathed physically but something had happened. I could tell. On his last leave, I asked him if he had seen too much in Vietnam.

He replied, "I saw too much in the first five minutes."

He, like Francie, believes in me. We are same blood. It doesn't help that he's on the other side of the world.

I drive back past the Cavalli ranch and the Seppi homestead. The highway carries me into town and I pull off and park by Dunn's Bar.

KOMA is playing Brown Sugar as I turn off the ignition and Jagger is rocking.

I should check myself in the rearview mirror but I don't care. I've grown up with everybody in the bar. They know me just like I know them. It all goes so deep in a small town--the love, the hate, the bickering, the gossip. Leadville takes it up a notch because of its isolation and year-round snows. At this altitude, most people can't breathe, let alone think. It makes for a stewpot of human emotions.

"Hey, Maddie!" yells Steve as I walk through the open door. We're used to the cold and we're all dressed for it. The place is full of hiking boots, jeans, flannel shirts and down vests. It's how we stay alive. We have each other's backs, especially with the violence that most of us face at home.

Steve is a true athlete, living for the game, his husky voice a trait he shares with all the siblings in his big Catholic family. He's blonde, with the classic Wadsworth nose, freckles and blue eyes.

"Hey, Steve." I sidle up to the group at the bar, acknowledging each of them. "Hi, guys. How's it going?"

"As crazy as ever," replies Steve.

I know his kisses. They are sweet and soft, with a gentle smile in between. But I wouldn't go past the kissing so it didn't last. They all know that. I only want the kissing. That's where I stop.

I know the girls are watching me. I notice that one of them has her fingers resting on Henry's arm.

"No," I think to myself. "Not Henry. You can do so much better. Don't go there." But she will do what she will.

Henry reminds me of some kind of animal but I can't put my finger on it. Maybe he's a fish, not a mammal at all. I've never touched him but I think he would feel cold. And wet. Slimy, even. His face is thin and long and something in his eyes is not right.

Henry leans into me, despite the touch from the other girl, and murmurs, "You look like you need some loving."

Wrong thing for him to say. Before I can check myself, I respond with a shove. The palm of my hand catches him at the collarbone and he falls back, grabbing for the bar.

He takes a menacing step toward me. Steve is quick to intercede, putting up his arm to block Henry and force him to step back.

"Hey, hey," says Steve with a disarming grin. "It's cool, man." He picks up Henry's beer and hands it to him. "To graduation," Steve says to the group, lifting his beer high in the air.

Henry hesitates but drinks to the toast, watching me with icy eyes.

I've made myself unattainable and I did it on purpose. Somehow I knew that sex too early would destroy me. From a young age, I had the knowledge that when I chose to walk through that door, it was going to change everything forever.

So I sidestepped and flirted and kept moving. I never stayed with one guy long enough for it to become an issue. I became a kissing connoisseur.

There's nothing I like more than the first kiss, the feeling of a warm, desiring mouth on mine. But it's always a dance, staying one step ahead of demands and expectations, floating light on my feet and keeping out of harm's way.

Nobody understood it. Not the boys. Not the girls. Rusty was the only one who knew what I was doing and why I was doing it.

"You want a beer?" asks Steve. He knows I don't but he's keeping it low-down.

"No, thanks. Just water," I reply.

Steve leans across the bar and yells, "Emil, regular for the lady!"

Down the bar, Emil tips his head amiably, looking through his pop-bottle glasses at me. His bald head reflects the overhead lights. Emil loves us. He has loved decades of us. He listens and he cares.

I smile at Steve, grateful that he understands. We dated for three weeks when we were sophomores. I remember his kiss and I know he remembers mine. He has a sweet smile. We will always be there for each other.

Chapter 4

Henry's anger is palpable but he continues to proposition me with his eyes, leading furiously with his eyebrows.

"Thanks, Emil," I say, avoiding Henry.

Emil sets my glass of water on the bar and pauses to talk. "Where are you headed, girl?"

"Working at the Opera House for the summer."

"Guiding tours again?"

I nod and take a drink of my water. Only for a while, I remind myself. I'm waiting for a response to the headshots I've sent out--a hundred of them. My secret.

And then?" he asks. "Are you staying?"

"No," I say, shaking my head. "Not staying. Kind of up in the air right now." I'm trying to stay cool and ambiguous.

"College?" Emil wipes down the bar.

"Probably," I lie. It's easier this way. "CSU."

"Gonna stay with the acting?"

Steve interjects. "Of course she is! Hollywood, hold onto your hats--Madelyn Tremaine is headed your way!"

Steve whoops, throwing his head back. My smile stiffens momentarily. He doesn't know how close he's come. I laugh to cover the catch in my breath.

Emil watches my face and reaches for my hand, speaking directly to me. "It's tough out there. You can always come home." He covers my hand with his.

I put my free hand on top, creating a pile of hands on the bar. I look at his wise, older face. "I know, Emil. This will always be home."

Steve slaps his hand on the top of the heap. "Leadville!" he yells.

The rest of the bar is attracted by Steve's volume and he yells it again. "Leadville!"

The bar takes it up as a chant. Steve bounces around the floor, leading the cheer. Since first grade, all us of have insisted that we were leaving Leadville as soon as we were able. Now, twelve years later, almost everybody is staying. Two are going to try college. One is going to beauty school in Pueblo for six months, living with her cousin. Three to the military.

It's a mining town. The mine claims almost everyone. Climax Molybdenum. Largest moly mine in the world. Good wages, hard work, strong union benefits. Hard to resist.

But the world is calling me. I can hear its siren song coming in on the wind. I wonder if Emil can hear it calling me too.

I glance back at him and he's watching me steadily. I give him a quick grin and whisper, "Leadville."

He nods, his eyes warm, and relinquishes my hand. There are glasses to fill.

I catch a scowl cross Henry's face. It's definitely time to move on.

I pick up my water glass and turn to stare down Henry. One thing I learned early was to never let them see me blink. I know that any display of vulnerability or weakness can get my teeth kicked in, physically or emotionally. Or both.

Henry breaks first, saying, "Okay, Miss Blue Eyes." He looks away, feigning indifference.

I smile and glance behind him, at the girl touching him. She has seen the exchange but doesn't know what to make of it. She doesn't know what to make of me.

I don't fit. It's one of the gifts of being a dork in junior high school. I didn't get imprisoned in a clique. I figured out more about myself than how to be social and popular.

I wander away from the bar, trailing Steve, who catches me in the middle of the floor and bear-hugs me.

"Don't you forget us," he whispers in my ear.

I'm not sure whether he means "us" from sophomore year or "us" as Leadville. Maybe both.

"Never," I whisper back.

He holds me for a moment, as if he wants it to last forever.

I like the way his body feels. The years of playing baseball have made him lean and sinewy. I like the hard closeness of his arms around me.

It would be easy to raise my mouth to his, to start it where we left off. We sway gently on the uneven floor. I can hear him humming to himself.

He's happy. I will leave it at that.

He gives me a final squeeze and whispers, "Maddie, Maddie," in my ear. He wanders back to the bar in search of another beer and I let him go.

Henry glares at him but Steve has a beer buzz going and doesn't notice. Henry's strategy was to isolate me and make me uncomfortable. But I'm too light on my feet for that.

I raise my water glass to him, smile at the girls, and join the cheerleaders. They giggle and scoot into the booth to make room for me. We discuss the upcoming talent show. They are performing a dance number. They are bubbly and excited.

I wonder what happens to cheerleaders twenty years down the line.

I slide to the next booth and talk high-mountain snow conditions with the ski team. They're planning to hike Mount Massive and ski down next week. I think about joining them. One last descent.

I pause to say hello to the shop guys, congratulating Terry on his new Header pipes. They envy me the Camaro and regularly invite me to race them at the straight-away by the golf course. Sometime I take them up on it. But not tonight.

It feels the way it has always felt except that every year the alcohol consumption has increased. So has their tendency to repeat themselves when drinking. I've spent years of my life listening to drinkers say the same thing over and over. Lost in the brew, hazy recollections, and the damnable sense of immediate importance.

I don't want to go home. There's nothing there for me. But I have school in the morning, one final day to put in, so I slide my water glass down the bar to Emil and wave goodbye.

Chapter 5

As I turn and take a step toward the door, I reach for the keys in my vest pocket and collide with an incoming Clyde. Clyde is 250 pounds of brawn and I bounce off him into a wobble. He catches me by the arms to set me straight.

"Whoa, there," he says with a grin. Clyde smiling is rare, but for some reason he became my protector some years ago, a self-appointed position that baffles me a little. Maybe it was the confusion, my general state of being, that signaled my need for protection. Maybe his tough shell hides a soft spot for lost puppies. I certainly am one.

I'm fazed from colliding with the brick fortress that is Clyde. Saying his name is all I can manage, "Clyde."

"You okay?" he asks, not letting go of my arms until he's sure I can stand on my own.

"Yeah," I respond. "I'm cool."

"I know you are," he laughs.

It's then I notice he's not alone. Another body stands behind him.

"Maddie, this is my cousin, Landry. From Pueblo." He steps aside.

I feel something change in the air before I look up. I can hear my heart pounding before I look into Landry's eyes. When I do, there's a shock of electricity between us.

I'm looking into the deepest, darkest eyes I've ever seen. A charged current makes the noise of the bar fall away. All I hear is a buzzing sound in my ears. I feel like I've been shot through with an arrow.

I'm having a hard time breathing.

His skin is smooth and poreless. He has the glossiness of a marble statue, a warm and dark marble statue. A heat radiates from him that pulls at me.

We stare at each other too long. Clyde doesn't say a word but I can tell he's watching. I know I need to break off the way I'm looking at this creature who has appeared before me but I'm powerless.

Whatever is happening, Clyde is a witness.

A smile twitches across Landry's lips. His mouth is strong and a delicate shading defines his lips.

Who is this guy? My peripheral vision has gone out and I reach for the bar. This is crazy.

"Hi," he says, his voice low and slow.

I notice his teeth and his tongue and I go weak in the knees. I've never seen anyone like this and he's standing in front of me, his eyes melting me.

"Hi," I hear myself say. Maybe I can muscle my way through this. Maybe I can hold myself together and not decompose into a gel on the floor of Dunn's Bar.

What the hell? Why can't I pull my eyes from this guy?

He has some kind of innocent darkness about him that is dissolving my backbone. He's standing there, one hand in his jacket pocket, and I'm sliding into oblivion.

Maybe I'm hemorrhaging internally from the collision, losing blood. Or maybe I hit my head without realizing it and I'm slipping into a coma. There's got to be a medical explanation for this.

"Don't leave, Maddie. Let me buy you a glass of water," says Clyde. He puts his hand on Landry's shoulder and Landry smiles at me again.

Shazam. That smile is like getting hit by lightning.

"You don't drink?" asks Landry.

I can't talk. Clyde answers for me, "Not a drop. Do you, Maddie?"

"No, no," I stammer.

"What do you do instead?" Landry asks.

"She acts," replies Clyde. "Girl's got talent in her toes."

"Acts? Like plays?" asks Landry.

"Yeah," says Clyde.

"But you don't drink?" repeats Landry. "That's interesting."

"Is it?" I hear myself say.

I find the bravery to reconnect with Landry's eyes. My heart still rattles around in my chest.

I watch as a smile slips across his silky lips. As his grin widens, I see those impossibly white, even teeth again. I'm in trouble. This one has something that I haven't encountered before.

He stands looking down at me and it's obvious that we both are caught in some kind of web. It's so obvious that Clyde laughs and slaps Landry on the shoulder. "Come on, big boy, let's get a beer. Maddie, can you join us?"

I smile lazily, trying to wade through the emotional avalanche that is carrying me. I'm held in place by unseen forces, magnetically glued to the spot. I can't walk away from this one. "Okay, one but then I've got to go."

Clyde and Landry order Coors in the bottle. Emil brings me another glass of water and sets it on the bar. The three of us find a booth.

They gesture me to slide in first. Clyde slips in beside me and Landry sits across. These are not their first beers of the evening. They are half-lit, slow and easy.

"You're from Pueblo?" I ask Landry.

"Yeah," he replies. "Graduated last year. Joining the Marines."

"Does that mean Vietnam?" I ask.

"Probably," he says, without hesitation. The war brings out a lot of mixed reactions and I'm sure he's heard his share of negative responses.

"My brother's done a tour in Nam. Navy," I tell him.

Clyde nods, "Her brother's a great guy. Kinda quiet but he's good." He turns to me, "How's he doing?"

"He's on the Kitty Hawk," I say, avoiding a discussion of my fears for my brother.

Landry raises an eyebrow, "Aircraft carrier."

"Yeah," I respond. "He works on Phantoms."

"How long's he been in?" asks Landry. He's interested and has every right to be. He's going to be landing there soon enough.

"Almost three years, one tour," I reply.

"Is he staying in?" he asks.

I pause. I don't know. Rusty's escape left me behind. He knew I was tough enough to do it on my own for two years. He was guessing. He couldn't stay here. Not even for me. So he left me the next-best thing: the Camaro.

But will he re-enlist? That's a subject we avoided on his leave. We sat on a rock at Gallagher's Ghost Mine late at night, watching the moon rise. He talked about the sea, the sound of the jets as they wind up for take-off, the friends who didn't make it back. I told him about my acceptance to

CSU, my senior-year classes, my part in Oklahoma.

I didn't tell him about my real plans and he didn't tell me whether he's going to re-enlist.

"I don't know," I say finally.

"It's a good life," Landry says.

I look at him. What is a good life? Do any of us know? Have we even tasted it? Caught a glimpse? Maybe we'll look back in thirty years, those of us who survive, and think that this was the best of times. I shudder involuntarily.

"You cold, girl?" asks Clyde.

"I'm always cold."

Landry laughs. "What kind of mountain girl are you?"

"Not a very good one," I admit.

"No," says Clyde, "This one's special. This one's really special."

"Thank you, Clyde," I say.

"I can see that," murmurs Landry, his words stirring the heat in my belly.

Where I am right now feels very slippery, an emotional glaze.

Although everyone teases me about my abstinence from alcohol and sex, there's a begrudging respect for it. Some are confounded and angered by it. I don't fit the model, their model. I don't really care. I'm finding my own way, pretty much blindly. Groping in the dark. Hoping for the best. Hoping for a break. A lot of my decisions are based on howling anxiety and fear.

But in a life where I've had so little control, so little autonomy, I've never wanted to give away what little power I did have. So I kept what I could and made myself fairly unattainable in the process. On purpose.

It's what has gotten me through in large part. No drunken black-outs for me. I've seen enough of that at home. No trading sweaty groping in someone's back seat for the fantasy of love. I've seen the price paid for that. Not a path I was willing to take.

I like being out of reach. But I want to kiss this guy, Landry, and I want him to kiss me back.

Chapter 6

The light-headed feeling does not subside. The booth is close and intimate and I can almost smell Landry. I want to put my nose against his neck and breathe in his scent. I want to climb across the table and kiss that mouth and pull his hair and somehow claim him as mine.

Fleetwood Mac launches into Black Magic Woman after finishing Dragonfly. Emil is playing the Greatest Hits tape.

""What time does graduation start?" asks Clyde, taking a drink of his beer.

His words jar me from my reverie. "What?" I stammer.

"You know, graduation? That thing at the end of high school?" Clyde laughs.

Landry asks, "You're graduating too?"

"Yes," I say. "Saturday morning. Ten o'clock."

"And what time is the talent show?" asks Clyde.

"There's a talent show?" asks Landry.

"Something the seniors are doing. It's going to be a lot of fun," I explain. "Clyde's band is playing."

"And you?" Landry poses the question.

"I'm doing a monologue. Opens the show."

"What's a monologue?" asks Landry.

"One-person play," I answer. And I tell him about the lineup of acts--the folk music, the cheerleader-dancers, Clyde's rock band.

"You're sticking around after graduation, aren't you, Landry? When are you leaving?" Clyde asks him.

I listen hard for the answer. When is he leaving? Which will provide an answer to the question bouncing in my brain--how long is he staying?

"Monday. Maybe Tuesday. I've got to be in San Diego on Thursday."

I have my answer. Five days. Maybe six, including tonight.

"It will be fun. Lots of good music," I encourage.

"And your play," adds Landry.

My heart skips a beat.

"You don't want to miss Maddie on stage," says Clyde, looking around for Emil to order another beer. "She's got something special going on."

I laugh,

Clyde continues. "This is the Maddie I talk about."

Landry looks at me. "You drive?"

"Does she drive? This is the one with the '69 Camaro," Clyde exclaims.

Landry looks back at me. "You're the girl who drives?"

"Yeah, I can drive," I reply. I can drive, there's no sense in denying it. The only person I've ever met who can outdrive me is Rusty.

Clyde is excited. "She does unbelievable stuff with that car. It's so cool. She lays it out, has an ear for the tach. Takes those corners so sweet, it fries your brain."

I laugh out loud. I've never heard driving described with such enthusiasm.

Clyde can't be stopped. "I don't know what she does in the curves. Nobody's ever seen anything like it. It's like she hunkers down on the drive train and floats the corners."

"My brother kind of invented it and we started working on it together," I explain to Landry.

Landry looks at me with cool calculation. He's assessing something and I can't tell what it is.

Clyde watches me too, his grin getting bigger by the second.

After a moment, I get it. "You want a ride?"

Clyde jumps up. "Yeah, yeah. The night is young. We need to go burn some rubber and tear up the high school parking lot."

I watch Landry as that smooth smile spreads across his lips. We are dancing, listening for the tune, swaying to the beat, circling tentatively without touching. And I'm about to get him in my Camaro.

Chapter 7

We leave the bar and pile into the car. Clyde climbs into the back seat, leaving the passenger seat for Landry. It confirms for me that Clyde is aware of the sparks between us.

"God, this is a car," says Landry appreciatively.

"I told you," replies Clyde.

My smile feels warm as I pull the seat belt across my lap. The car fires up and Clyde whistles at the sound of the glass-pack pipes.

"Cool," he proclaims.

I glance at Landry and realize he has been watching me set up to drive. American Woman hits the speakers from Oklahoma City.

Landry leans back and closes his eyes for a moment. I can't tell what he's thinking.

"Let's do it!" shouts Clyde, drumming his hands on the back of Landry's seat.

I take the side streets to the high school parking lot. The conversation is loud and happy. It feels good to be young and in a bright red Camaro. It doesn't hurt that I have a great friend in the back seat and a beautiful brown-eyed boy in the seat beside me.

The Milky Way looks like a laceration across the sky. The snow has gone except for the high mountains. It's almost summer in the high country. Graduation is around the corner and I have plans. Big plans. Plans that give me wings. Plans that scare me half to death.

"You hear the power under that hood?" asks Clyde of Landry.

Landry whistles low and slow. "This is a fine machine."

I smile and glance at him through my eyelashes. He's beautiful and I know how to flirt. I love to flirt. Nobody loses and everyone wins. All parties walk away feeling special, desired and happy.

But flirting slips so easily into something heavier. That's when it ceases to be flirting. It loses its genuineness and its lightness and becomes something greasy and dirty. There's no grace or creativity to sexual innuendo. It doesn't do anything for anyone. Henry is a perfect example. That stuff makes me want to go home and take a shower. It makes my skin crawl.

I'm hoping Landry does not take it there. I'm hoping he knows the wisdom of lightness and grace. The dance is what I want. Frivolous, fluffy and sweet.

"She's got wings, for sure," I respond. I'm talking as much about myself as the car. This machine is my baby, my ultimate connection with Rusty, and I love it when someone appreciates her.

Clyde finds my 8-track case in the back seat and gleefully looks through it.

"Ooooh," he yells. He picks a Led Zeppelin tape and hands it to me to play. I push it into the slot and Jimmy Page moves into Immigrant Song.

"We come from the land of the ice and snow..." he wails.

Landry leans back in his seat and enjoys the opening of the song. "Doesn't get any better than this," he says.

"You got that right," agrees Clyde.

I drop the clutch and reach for the gear shift as we roll into the parking lot at the high school.

Landry notices that I'm readying and moves his knee away from the shifter. I smile at him and he smiles back.

I slide into an easy doughnut, spinning loose rock and smoking the tires.

Clyde hoots in the back seat. I see Landry reaching for something to brace himself. I don't say a word. When I get the full 360 degrees, I flick the steering wheel and send the car in the other direction--all the way around, coming out of the circle without jerking.

"Atta girl," yells Clyde. He has been with me before and he knows what the car and I are capable of. "Take it out, sister!"

I slide through another 360 in a counter-clockwise direction. Landry starts laughing. His laugh hits me at gut level and I feel a twisting and lifting that comes up through my heart and into my throat.

Landry is right--it doesn't get any better.

"It's a 307 V-8—a 327 crank in a 283 block," I shout to Landry over the music and the sound of the car's performance.

Landry nods, "Impressive."

Clyde hoots from the backseat again as I take the car into a long slide. It feels like we're skimming the surface of the parking lot sideways. I put the Camaro through another series of figure-eights and head out of the parking lot before the noise attracts the police.

Clyde stops hollering and leans his head back to breathe. He pipes up with an idea, "Let's go to Strawberry Fields!"

I glance over at Landry and he seems game for anything, saying, "The night is young."

Clyde agrees, "Hell, yeah!"

So we cruise east, laughing, enjoying the night and each other.

Chapter 8

Landry and I lie on the stage at the Tabor Opera House, looking up into the catwalk, the profusion of lights and the beautiful but aged hand-painted drops. I switched on two dim cone lights so the stage is bathed in pools of darkness.

The building is not open yet for the season but I used my key and brought Landry with me. I need to be here tonight. Our heads are beside each other and our feet facing in opposite directions. The stage floor is dirty but we don't care.

The three of us stayed out late last night, wandering around Strawberry Fields in the darkness, illuminated as a cold moon rose over the mountains. We built a small fire but didn't stay long.

I took them home at midnight. When I pulled up in front of Clyde's house, Landry stepped out of the car and Clyde climbed out of the back seat, nuzzling my cheek.

Landry leaned back in and said, "I…"

He didn't say any more. It was like he couldn't. He looked at me with those pooling, liquid eyes.

The fire between us was intense and I could hear my heart pounding. "I know," I said, my heart in my throat. I lightly asked, "Would you like to see the Opera House tomorrow?"

Landry paused and smiled. He nodded his head and said, "Yes, I would."

These are the last days of school--winding it down. Ticking off the hours. It's been a flurry of signing yearbooks, picking up graduation gowns and wandering in a lost way through the halls, making final contacts and touching things for the last time–the gym bleachers, the cafeteria tables, the graffiti in the bathrooms.

For some reason we are touching everything, like kindergarteners re-experiencing everything in a tactile way. We do not trust our other senses to remember.

Landry tucks one hand under his head as he talks. He's telling me about his biological father-- the one he's never met. "He's a boxer," he says.

"A boxer?" I repeat, thinking about Landry's big hands. Maybe he inherited them.

"Yeah, in California. But my mom divorced him before I was born."

"Couldn't keep the violence in the ring?" I ask boldly.

"You got it." He's fine answering my question.

I like that.

"You've never met him?" I ask.

"No. No contact," he says.

"Is that okay with you?"

"Not really my choice. But it's cool, I guess. Just the way it is," he finishes.

"You're going to be in California..." I remind him.

"Haven't really thought about it. My stepdad, Leo, is my dad," Landry says. "He raised me since I was three."

"You're lucky to have him."

"Yeah, I am. Leo and my mom had more kids. So I've got two brothers and three sisters," he says.

"Big family," I observe.

"Yeah, do you have any besides your brother?"

No, it's just the two of us now." I know where this goes.

"Now?" He caught it.

"I had another brother."

"What happened to him?"

"He disappeared," I say as simply as I can.

"What do you mean? He's dead?"

"Don't know. Vanished. Poof," I say. "On his way home from ski team practice one night."

"They never found him?"

"Not a trace."

Landry pauses, thinking it through. "How long ago?"

"Five years. He was the oldest. His name is Joel."

Landry sits up and leans over to look into my eyes. He doesn't say anything.

I feel the way I always do when I talk about Joel. It's like falling--everything slows down and the sound of it is empty, hollowed-out, flat.

"Like you said, it's just the way it is," I say.

Landry rolls onto his back. "That's a tough one."

We lie quietly for a while. I'm waiting for the feeling to come back into my arms and legs--my body always goes numb when I think about Joel.

I remember living it like a nightmare. Everything fell apart. There was no more pretending, no more holding up the threadbare appearances we had maintained for years. It collapsed under its own weight.

And I know, as I always do when I tell the story, that Landry needs a few moments to digest what I've told him. They always do. It's freaky and I know it.

I can't think of anything to say. I extend my arms toward the ceiling three stories above, using my hands to frame sections of the technical hardware above the Opera House stage.

Landry watches my movements.

I speak first. "Houdini appeared on this stage."

"Yeah?"

"The trap door was built for him."

"Makes sense. Quite a place," he says.

"Haunted."

"Really?"

"Yup. Lady in white appears on that balcony." I point. We both peer into the darkness but she doesn't materialize.

"Two years ago we found a ventriloquist's dummy sealed in a room downstairs. All by itself." I tell him.

"Who put it there?"

"Who knows? I answer. "Looked like it had been there for sixty, seventy years."

"Weird."

"Yeah. And after we let him out, strange things started happening."

"Like what?"

"Accidents--sprained ankles, broken arms, cars rolling off cliffs when the emergency brake was on."

"Because the dummy was out?"

"Or coincidence. We took him out in the woods and burned him."

"Crazy shit."

"Things got better after we killed him."

A silence follows. So much for small talk.

Since we're in so deep, I say what's on my mind. "Why the Marines?"

"Pride?" he ventures.

"There's a war on."

"Yeah. And whatever happens, happens."

I sigh and look over at him, dropping my hands to my stomach. "Do you think you'll be career?"

It's his turn to sigh. "Right now I think so. Been a little bonkers lately. I need to do this. I need to get my head screwed on."

"I'm not sure going to Vietnam is going to help with that. My brother's been there and doesn't have much good to say about it."

"Did he see any action?" asks Landry. He turns his head and our eyes meet.

My heart jumps.

"Not sure. It changed him."

Landry opens his mouth to say something but closes it and turns to stare back at the catwalk. I do the same.

"Maybe they won't send me there," he says.

"Maybe."

Neither of us believes it. It hovers over all of us, the entire generation, like a rain-soaked blanket. It's always there. It dampens everything, heavy and smelling like wet wool.

All the young men have their draft number scarred on the inside of their brain, like concentration camp numbers on the last generation's wrists.

Chapter 9

I get up. I walk downstage and turn back to look at Landry lying on the floor. His eyes watch me.

"There's a part in the play, the monologue…"

"Meteor Shower? Is that the name of it?" asks Landry.

"Yes, Meteor Shower."

"Mmmmm," he says, watching me.

I recite the lines, moving into character. "When I was little, I loved to climb trees, the higher the better. Way up in the sky. I never wanted to come down. To what? Swaying in the wind, so far about the ground, I was invisible."

Landry listens without saying anything, and when I'm done, he stays quiet, watching me. My words hover in the silence.

Finally he says, "Yeah. Clyde is right. You're good."

"Will you be there tomorrow?" As soon as I say it, I wish I could take it back. It exposes me. It sounds vulnerable, needy.

"For sure," laughs Landry. "Clyde's playing in the band and you're doing your thing."

"My graduation present."

"Present?"

"My favorite teacher wrote it for me. Francie Wilbur. Makes it special."

"I can see that."

I look up at the light so far above us shining down on an empty spot on the stage. "She's one of those teachers who changes lives."

"I never had one of those." He's still watching me.

"I'm sorry."

"For what?"

"Everyone needs an amazing teacher," I say. I've had two.

We continue to look at each other. There's something there. I feel it. He feels it. Clyde sensed it last night.

Landry's new to me. There's something exciting and comfortable about it. Time falls away and is not applicable. If it was matter, it would be suspended matter. If it was energy, it would create disruptions as profound as solar flares.

The talking keeps it light, makes it manageable. It's a foil. It buys us time. We need time, even when there isn't any, even when the hours on the clock melt into a pile of numbers on the mantle, on the floor of the classroom, on the arch at City Hall. A melted pile of numbers, dissolving the definition of time.

I don't know how long we stare at each other. Fifteen seconds, fifteen years, it makes no difference.

I'm a sucker for falling in love. I've never let it last more than a month because of the inevitable pressures about sex. It's my intoxication. It's my addiction. I want it to be young and pure and unbridled by any bullshit. This is the way I want it to be, staring at each other, touching each other's souls across the expanse of a stage of a hundred-year-old Opera House in the semi-dark with no noise.

Chapter 10

Neither of us speaks. It's getting late and tomorrow is the last day of school for me. I don't want to be the one who breaks the spell but Landry's gaze is not wavering.

I sigh and look away. I hate to do it because it signifies a loss of power. Power is what I'm after, always, in every situation. It's the only place I can find safety. I learned so many years ago, as a child in a violent family in a violent town, all about power and control—its uses and abuses.

It's almost midnight. We've touched on some tricky and tentative subjects. I know I'm not what he's used to. I'm not what anyone's used to.

"It's late," I say, calling it.

"It's late," he repeats and sits up, bending one blue-jeaned leg to stand.

I shut down the light board. Landry watches the process on the relic and says, "Thanks for the tour."

I smile and reply, "A very unofficial one. You'll have to come back for a real tour next week."

"Next week. Yeah, I'll do that," he says. We are both acutely aware of where he will be next week. "I'd like to see you in costume"

"I know everything there is to know about this place."

"Everything?"

"I know where the ghosts are."

"Should I be looking for the lady in white?" he queries.

"No. I don't feel her tonight."

"The spirits are quiet?" he intones.

"Never really quiet. That's why they're here. Unfinished business."

"Come on. You're starting to freak me out," he says suddenly.

"Yeah?" I say, crossing my arms defensively. "Sorry."

"Just all this death stuff."

"Okay, I'll go easy on you and not tell you about the ghosts on the top floors." I take off up the aisle, leaving him in the dark. He catches me at the top seats and spins me around, looking into my eyes.

He's aching to kiss me. It's all over his face. He moves into me, backing me into the wall. He hasn't taken his eyes from me and I cannot tear my gaze from him.

He leans one elbow into the wall by my head and puts his other hand around my neck. His lips are warm and demanding when he kisses me. I close my eyes and feel the swoon begin. Everything happening between us is concentrated in the kiss.

He kisses me again and I feel his hand travel up my neck to my hair. He gathers it like a rope and pulls it over my shoulder.

He leans away from me, holding my hair, and looks away. "It's late," he says.

I smile. He has looked away first this time. We are even.

His touch has made me tingle all the way down my spine to my toes. The smell of his skin carries a heat. He smells clean and warm. His body is so smooth and flawless that my body aches.

I want more but he has blinked. He has pulled back and I can now reclaim the power that I gave up earlier on the stage. I smile flirtatiously and peck him quickly on the cheek. It sets a tone. It lets him know that I liked it.

I already know it's not going to be easy. He's as intense and angry as I am. I know he feels the way I do. We are being very tentative with each other because the anger is raw and fragile. We are dancing, like two big cats circling, knowing the future is up for grabs for both of us. In weeks or months, nothing will be as it is now. It is exciting and terrifying.

Chapter 11

When I drop off Landry at Clyde's house, he kisses me again, sweetly, wholly, with lightness and caring. Driving home, I'm infused with his kisses.

There, I walk into Hell. I don't know why my parents are back together.

The divorce was final three years ago. He moved out. She got a boyfriend. He got a girlfriend. Then he had multiple girlfriends and bragged on visitations about keeping them juggled. My mother stopped drinking. Then she started drinking again. My father never even tried.

They are screaming obscenities at each other when I walk in the door. They pause and glower at me for upsetting the syncopation of the argument.

I grab a glass of milk and lock myself in my bedroom. My graduation gown hangs on the closet door, the mortar board on my desk. I open my closet, assessing how long it will take to box up all the contents. It's almost warm enough to move into the tree house.

Rusty and I built the tree house four years ago, after Joel disappeared. It's in the pine forest behind the cemetery. It was our escape from the wanton craziness that erupted at home. Sometimes we lived in the tree house for days at a time before venturing back to see what destruction had ensued in our absence. It's as tight and high as we could get it but the nights were always bitterly cold.

The fighting starts again from the living room, the seething hatred mixed up with alcohol and the lateness of the hour.

"Goddamn it, Myrtle," I hear my father hiss.

"Go to hell, Earl," is my mother's response.

I hear him kick something--a door or the wall. "I just asked you for a beer."

"Get it yourself, asshole."

"Why can't I get any respect in my own goddamn house?" he bellows.

"It's not your goddamn house!"

If I can get through graduation and the talent show tomorrow, I can move to the tree house. I can shower at the Opera House in the mornings. I can cook on the camping stove. There's no electricity so I won't have refrigeration but canned soup is better than this.

I pause and realize that we haven't had a sit-down meal in five years.

"This is what I mean, you bitch. How do you think this makes me feel?" my father roars.

"I don't care how it makes you feel. This is not your goddamn house," my mother yells back.

Something hits the wall--probably a lamp.

I rented a box at the post office. It's my return address for the headshots, the applications I sent out--each one a dart of hope in the darkness. Choose me. Let me try. Give me a chance.

"I don't know why in hell I ever came back here," my father curses.

"I don't either. I never asked you to. You did it on your own, damn you," my mother shrieks back.

"This place stinks. What kind of a mother are you to let your daughter live in this pigsty?"

I went to the tree house last week and swept it out, pulling down an old bird's nest and checking for tracks to see if anyone had discovered the hideaway. It looked clear, traces of melting snow still softening the ground. I need to fill the propane for the camping stove. And I need to leave this house forever.

"What kind of a father are you letting your son disappear?" I hear my mother scream in response, storming down the hall and slamming the door to her bedroom.

My father starts kicking things and settles on the couch, heavily, drunkenly. He will be sitting there in the morning, head thrown back, snoring loudly, the stench of alcohol permeating the room.

I review my escape plan. There's a warren of rooms upstairs at the Opera House where I could stay but only occasionally. The tree house is my best option.

I hear my father cursing loudly from the couch. "Piss me off. Who does she think...what the hell am I even doing here? Putting up with this shit?" He will fall asleep sooner or later.

I touch my lips, feeling Landry's kiss all over again. The heat of his mouth was everything I'd hoped it would be. There's a fire in my belly as I pull the pillow over my head, blocking the street light outside my window and muffling the curses from the other side of the wall.

Chapter 12

In the morning, I shower quickly and leave for school. Except for my father's snores from the bedroom, indicating a reconciliation of sorts, the house is silent. A lamp is broken and there is a foot-sized hole in the TV screen. The one device that helped stabilize the volatility in the house is now out of commission.

School is humming. Everyone is excited and the seniors, me included, are slightly dazed and itching to get on with it. It's a frenzied scene as our class enters the auditorium for a final debriefing.

"If everyone will take a seat!" comes Francie's voice over the sound system as I enter. She's standing on stage, holding the microphone, gesturing to accentuate her command.

I find Bette and sit by her in the auditorium. She's three months pregnant. I know. Her boyfriend knows. She had an abortion last year, our junior year. It was a different boyfriend a year ago.

It's all part of the reason for my choices about sex. I don't want to walk that path. I'm following a different road.

"Let's get started. First, congratulations!" Francie proclaims. "Class of 1971, you did it!"

We cheer. Francie is a senior class advisor so one of her duties is corralling 112 of us through the final days here.

I don't know what Bette is going to do. We have discussed it, at lunch, after school. Waiting is a decision in itself.

"The easy stuff first--be sure to turn in your library books," Francie announces. "Get initials to prove it."

Everyone feels rowdy, cheering wildly for no reason other than joy as Francie makes each announcement.

Bette didn't want the abortion last year. She was scared and bullied into it. Mama Rose was determined, despite the Catholicism, the cost and the gossip, that her daughter was going to have better than a repeat of her life.

"Turn in your textbooks and verify that you've completed your work for each class. Get the initials, people."

This statement is met with heady applause and whistling. We are having so much fun counting it down.

I see the future of so many of the girls--too many children, not enough money, abuse and alcohol, hard jobs, broken bodies and early deaths. What is it about small towns? In books and on TV, parents always talk about moving to small towns to give their children a quality life. Maybe. Just not Leadville.

It's the children of Leadville who make it a magical place. Early on we learn to watch each other's backs, to find the goodness in life away from the various cruelties of home.

We spend every minute we can removed from the family nest. We ski, we hike, we raft, we camp, we talk around bonfires. We laugh at football games, yell our hearts out at basketball games and wrestling matches. We are all we have and we know it. We are the family unit-- parents need not apply.

"Clean out your lockers. Anything left behind goes to the dump. Gym lockers too."

I still feel Landry's kisses on my lips. I feel his hands on my neck and in my hair. I can smell his skin, so close, taunting my senses, taunting my heat. The memory is so strong I close my eyes.

Bette hears me take a sharp breath and elbows me. "What are you doing?"

"Nothing," I whisper back. I return my attention to the stage.

Francie is the second teacher who helped me through. Ned Blair was the first. He found me in seventh grade, inviting me to join Scribblers, the school writing club. He helped me find my voice, not only on paper but verbally. He loved turning the club meetings into reader's theater. I was up for anything he and his world could bring to me. I was a lonely outcast; he helped me not care. He was an eccentric epileptic who belonged in the last century. He loved history, always wearing clothes to match.

I wrote poetry for him until I breathed poetry. I dreamed poetry. I practiced the part of Eliza Doolittle until my reader's theater performance didn't need to be read.

I fantasized about marrying him since I was abjectly and thoroughly in love with him. He was my knight in shining armor. When I was in ninth grade, he went off and married a tall, willowy radio announcer. I was crushed. Devastated and crimson red, I don't know how I got through the Scribblers meeting when he announced it. It had never crossed my mind that he could love anyone but me.

There were so many times, places in the stream, where I could have gone so wrong. Or maybe I'm fooling myself. Maybe I'm sordidly wrong and don't even know it. Maybe the damage runs so deep and I'm so oblivious to it that I'm a serial killer in waiting, a delusional nut-job who will spend the rest of my life locked up in Pueblo or a mother of eleven on welfare and heroin. Such are the choices that lay before me, a smorgasbord of ruthlessness.

"Graduation gowns must be turned in immediately after graduation. Get the pictures taken, put your gowns and mortarboards on the table. And go live."

Chapter 13

Bette and I walk out of the auditorium, our heads full of our own situations but fully instructed. She looks weak and white, suddenly sitting at a cafeteria table.

"You okay?" I ask.

"No. I feel like shit."

"What can I do?"

"Just shut up."

I love Bette's snarky mouth. I've always loved it. Being only 5'1", she can get away with it--the sarcasm, the funny put-downs. Anyone over 5"4" would get her face smashed in.

"I'm getting married next week," she states flatly.

"Where?"

"Salida. The courthouse. The start of a whole new life. Away from my mother. Forever." She's definite.

The summer of Woodstock, two years ago, I proposed that we go. Take off for upstate New York and be part of something bigger than Leadville, Colorado. It didn't happen.

This year I advanced a plan to move to Denver after graduation, finding an apartment and jobs as secretaries.

She's always been just outside my grasp.

I'm losing her for real this time and I know it. She keeps fading into her relationships, growing dimmer and dimmer as her light goes out. She's still there but not there.

The boyfriends drain her of something and I'm powerless to change it. I see her path and I want to yank her off of it but she's as steadfast and stubborn as I am.

"Do you want me there?" I ask.

"No. We'll get witnesses from wherever--the hall, I guess."

"Have you told Rose?"

"Good Lord, no. She'd tie me to the chimney in the attic with light cords."

I pause. "She probably would."

She looks down at her hands.

"Are you sure?" I ask gently. I mean about everything--witnesses, marriage, pregnancy, sex, the whole menagerie that makes up a life.

"Yup," she says, her mouth set hard but her eyes full of fear. "I'm sure."

"I'll be here for you. You know that," I say after a while.

"Until you leave for college."

Should I tell her? I haven't breathed a word to anyone. I could just say it. Instead I say, "Yeah. College."

"Better you than me," she says, her chin jutting forward in the display of stubbornness I know so well. "I would hate college," she lies bravely.

There's so much I want to tell her--about Landry, about driving to Denver and having the headshots made up, about my alternative plans.

But she has a baby in her belly and a secret wedding next week. I decide I'll keep it to myself. A while longer.

Chapter 14

When Bette gets her feet under her, we forge ahead on our appointed rounds, procuring the initials required to graduate.

At lunchtime Bette, Clyde and I climb in the Camaro and head downtown to the bakery. Annie Walker makes the best bread in the world.

I can eat it by the handful and be totally satisfied. There's something about the aroma, the earthiness and dusting of flour, the texture of the crust and the sweet softness of the inside. It's a hedonistic experience in its own right.

We sit on the sidewalk in front of the bakery watching the traffic on Harrison Avenue, feeling content. I'm still warm from Landry's kisses and perfectly happy.

I suddenly miss Landry. My heart lurches and I choke on my bread.

"You gettin' her?" asks Clyde, pounding me on the back.

"No. I think I'm going to die," I respond, tears filling my eyes.

"Want a drink?" asks Bette, offering her soda.

I shake my head and grab Clyde's arm so he stops hitting me.

"Let her die," snipes Bette. "We'll tell people we tried everything."

I laugh. Clyde joins in. Soon we are gasping for breath on the sidewalk. Everything seems so funny. I'm sitting on the concrete with my pregnant best friend and the vocalist for The

Grilled Cheese Incident, not knowing anything, nothing at all, and I can't stop laughing.

The afternoon is spent in chaos in the gym. We are rehearsing but what we are really rehearsing is the pandemonium we feel in our hearts and our heads.

"People, it's got to be alphabetical!" Francie instructs for the grand march.

"And don't forget the initials!" yells Steve, who is balancing on the bleachers attempting an arabesque.

His right leg is shaking from the effort and his left leg lashes the air as he kicks into position. A fall is imminent. I jump on the bleachers and face him, grabbing his forearms to support him. He smiles at me and I wink.

Together we move into ballet position, a double arabesque with attitude, undoubtedly the most ballet ever performed in the high school gym, at least on the bleachers.

The gym erupts into applause and Steve swings his leg out of its ridiculous positioning and into a deep squatting plié. I do the same. He dips into another plié. I repeat, completing a syncopated bobbing.

"Well done, Steve, Maddie," quips Francie on the microphone. "You've learned useful life skills."

Chapter 15

The final bell of our high school careers rings, loud and insistent, hammering in our ears for the last time. We are done. It's over. The textbooks are turned in, the lockers are cleaned out, and the school ejects us like a purge. We are done.

Not waiting for anyone, I race out the door, heading straight for the parking lot. I see Landry, leaning against my car, arms crossed. I wasn't expecting to see him. Not there, waiting for me. My heart stalls.

I'm wearing boots, and inanimate objects though they may be, they pick up the pace. I'm careening, my blue-jeaned legs stretching out. I'm covering a lot of ground.

He sees me and smiles but I cannot reduce my speed. He raises his arms when he realizes I'm not stopping and the look on his face makes my heart jump. I slam into his chest and he exaggerates an "Ooomph."

I tilt my chin up and close my eyes and he obliges me. He thoroughly kisses me. His arms lock around me and he pulls me in tight, eliminating all the space between us. We are molded together and I hold his face in my hands, devouring his kisses until we are both weak and breathless.

"Whoa there, cowboy," comes a voice from behind me. It's Bette, hoping to catch a ride home. Her tone is appreciative and surprised. There has been no time to tell her about Landry.

"And who might you be, smooching on my friend?" Bette says to Landry.

I have trouble catching my breath. It happens every time Landry touches me. He kisses me like it might be the last chance he has. He kisses me like he's memorizing me. He kisses me like he's going to Vietnam and has no idea what awaits him there.

"I'm Landry. Clyde's cousin." He reaches out to shake Bette's hand but doesn't let go of me.

I try to focus on Bette but my eyes won't align. I look up at the dappled sky, the puffs of clouds set off by the furious blue. I can feel Landry's heart pounding in his chest. Mine is louder.

I know I should say something but there's no sound in me.

Bette asks him curtly, "Does your mother know where you are?"

Landry laughs and the vibration in his chest tingles against my ribs. He relinquishes the handshake and wraps me in close again.

"Not really, I guess," he answers.

"Well, maybe you should run along and check in with her," snaps Bette, her eyes twinkling with the fun of it.

"And you are..." enquires Landry.

I know I have to find words. I'm standing mute and senseless.

"Bette," she retorts. "Surely you've heard of me."

"Landry," I say slowly, trying to form the words in my mouth, the mouth that Landry has just kissed the words from. "This is my friend, Bette."

Bette turns to me. "A little late on the uptake, don't you think, cupcake?"

Clyde lopes into view. "Better late than never! Hey, Bette, have you met my cousin--?"

Bette snaps, "Of course I have. I should have known he was related to you."

Clyde is clueless. Bette has that delivery. I start to giggle at the confused look on Clyde's face. Landry is enjoying the exchange. I like the way he's rolling with it.

It's the second time today my situation has tickled me. I'm fluttery inside and know what that means. It's what I live for--that combination of lifting and falling. It's a weightlessness I crave.

"Yeah, my cousin," says Clyde, looking around. "Did I miss something?"

"Only your cousin macking on my best friend," answers Bette.

"Oh, that," counters Clyde. "Yeah, that's been happening."

"Really?" asks Bette, looking directly at me. "And how long has this little idyll been going on?"

Clyde pretends to take her seriously. "I don't know. Two days? Three? When did you get here, Landry?"

Landry laughs and gives me a light embrace. "Where you headed, cupcake?" he asks, using Bette's designation for me.

"To hell in a hand basket, from the look of things," wisecracks Bette. "Can I get a ride home?" she asks me.

"Sure," I reply. "You don't want to celebrate?"

"No, Rose is rampaging and I'm supposed to get home and start dinner," Bette says. She has always called her mother Rose.

Most of us call our parents by their first names. They never earned any other label. And if they ever did, they lost it along the way.

"We're meeting at The Circle. Maddie?" asks Clyde.

I glance at Landry and he nods, releasing me. "Meet you there?"

I nod.

Landry kisses me, slowly, luxuriously, inviting me into his world. And I do want to go there.

Bette clucks, a perfect imitation of her mother. "Spaghetti and meatballs. Don't skimp on the garlic."

We laugh. I break from Landry's grasp and feel for my keys. I reach back and run my finger across Landry's beautiful lips. There's a promise of more. His eyes blaze me with desire. I want more.

We leave Landry and Clyde discussing whether to take Landry's Buick or Clyde's Jeep. Bette slides into the passenger seat and pats the dash.

"Good girl," she says to the car.

Then she turns to me. "Can't say the same for you."

"No?"

"Spill it," she orders.

"He showed up. For Clyde's graduation. On his way to the Marines."

"Oh, shit," wails Bette softly. "What the hell did he do that for?"

My thoughts pass to Rusty. There's been no word in three weeks. Walter Cronkite announces the casualties every night on CBS but it's not enough information. It's happening half a world away.

During the day I stop and try to sense Rusty over the distance, like I did when Joel vanished. Sometimes I can catch something, a shift in sound, a jump in the light. Most of the time there's nothing.

I say nothing.

"I bet he didn't know you were going to walk into his life," Bette goes on. "Must have bowled him right over."

"There's something about him."

"Uh oh," warns Bette. "How far has this gone?"

How far? I ask myself. Emotionally, I feel like I've skipped across a galaxy or two.

"Kissing."

"Is he good?"

I glance knowingly at her. "Amazing."

"He looks like he'd be good. He sure is pretty."

"He's--a looker," I'm still short on words. It goes far beyond appearance and I don't know how to explain it. There's a heat about him. The buzz in my brain when I'm with him, like I can hear my own blood.

"Yeah," says Bette with emphasis. I'm glad she appreciates what I've been feasting my eyes on for the past few days.

"He's not here for long."

"That's too bad," empathizes Bette. "I'm sure you'd figure out something to do with him."

"He's pretty cool," I sum up as I stop the car across the street from her house. I don't want to pull in the driveway. There's no sense getting too close to Rose and her eternal ire. Across the street is close enough.

Bette reaches for her backpack, heavy with locker contents. "You look good together. Have fun tonight. Don't do anything I wouldn't do."

"Doesn't limit me much, does it?"

"No, not much at all."

I grin as she shakes her head. She gets out of the car and hefts the backpack onto her shoulder.

"Thanks," she says. She crosses the street, looking back as she reaches the gate.

What I want more than anything in the world is for her to find happiness but there's a weight like a rock in the bottom of my stomach. I blow her a kiss as she opens the gate.

Chapter 16

I drive up Sixth Street and turn right at the light. It's a one traffic-light town. I know I'm supposed to meet Clyde and Landry but I stop at the Opera House instead. I lock the door behind me, climbing the grand staircase, the walls lined with old photographs and playbills. The steps creak under my boots.

I open the doors to the theater and switch on a few lights. I address the stage.

"Horace. Baby Doe."

They are here, all these years later. I can feel them. I can sense the intensity they had. From humble beginnings both—Horace raised in Vermont and a shopkeeper; Baby Doe born in Oshkosh, Wisconsin to Irish immigrants.

"I will become more than I am expected to be," I tell their ghosts, reciting from the play.

"I will not allow my confines to be my limitation." The words from Meteor Shower settle on the stale air.

Theirs is a rags-to-riches-to-rags story that speaks to me. They are a part of me. Their history pulses under my skin. Baby Doe survived a violent first marriage to marry again for passion and money.

I look up at the Tabor box, where Horace and Baby Doe sat and watched the spectacle of the theater unfold, the respect and jealousy of their neighbors laid out like a carpet below them.

I wander down the aisle and enter the stage door. I gaze up at the ropes, lines and wires dangling overhead, as ready as they were a hundred years ago to delight the minds of the audience. To make the magic happen. To lower the drops and change the lighting to lead the senses somewhere other than the hard-scrabble lives of Leadville.

I whisper to the building, to the ghosts, a line from the play. "But I can use all the luck you're inclined to wish me."

I pause at the spot on the stage where Landry and I lay last night. I don't know if we actually created a disturbance in the dust, or whether we left a thermal imprint, but I know exactly where we were.

I walk the stage, checking the electric cords and microphones.

Oscar Wilde walked this stage. He loved reading poetry to the rough, hardened miners of Leadville. Tallulah Bankhead trilled to the crowd in the balcony, setting things on a different note, like a songbird, for a few moments in time.

There's no place like Leadville anywhere on earth.

I think through the last line of Meteor Shower and feel myself drop into character.

"I guess I'll be seeing you."

My breathing deepens and flattens, as it always does when I hook into my character. I feel her, the character of Tammy, in every inch of my body. I know who she is and why she is. I say the line and it rings in my head with the same clarity that the sound makes in the theater.

Then I whistle. I whistle as I leave the stage and walk down the stairs to the aisle. I whistle as I walk up the aisle and turn out the lights.

And I get it. I fully comprehend the end of the play.

Chapter 17

When I first looked at the script, I wasn't sure how the whistling would play. But it symbolizes something that is wordless but auditory, melodic but not really musical. I haven't seen the effect on an audience, but hearing the sound of whistling in that grand old theater, even empty, is haunting. Tomorrow night I will know.

The place will be full. The town will be watching me onstage one last time.

They won't know I'm standing on the edge of a cliff. Out of breath, out of options, I hear the demons gaining on me.

Which is why, one day in March, I skipped school and travelled over Loveland Pass, making my way into Denver, posing and paying for a series of photographs that were enameled onto glossy paper, paper that carried all my future dreams out into the world.

I mailed one to Rusty. I sent it to his ship, a mailbag address. My pictures are traveling the world to reach him and that gives me a sense of momentum. It's the feeling of flying into the future that I get when I jump the Camaro from third to fourth, sailing gear. It's the same sense I get when I come out of tight curves into a straightaway and the Camaro never hesitates. She gives and gives and gives, no lag, no hesitation.

If the letter comes, when the letter comes, I will load up all I own in the world and head out of Leadville in the magnificent machine that bides her time at the curb.

Landry is waiting a few miles away, in a grove newly sprung from ice and snow. I can feel my body homing in on him. I picture the glance that sends a light arrow into my heart. I feel the warmth of his lips on my neck and the tightness of his arms when he pulls me close.

I give the Camaro her head like a fiery horse. And she flies to Landry, to the party waiting in the woods, the laughter, the intimacy of the joking, the end and beginning.

Chapter 18

When I pull up to The Circle, the bonfire burns high and hot. My schoolmates mill around, drinking beer from paper cups filled at the keg.

The sun is shining but it has been a cool day. I slide out of the car, realizing that it's cold enough to snow tonight. There's a chill in the air that will make the heat from the fire most welcome.

I see Landry immediately, leaning against Clyde's car, his back to me. Debbie has planted herself in front of him and she's chattering at him. Debbie chatters at everyone. I don't know if she's flirting or being friendly but I can tell from Landry's posture that he's not connecting with her.

He glances over his shoulder and sees me. I see him stop Debbie with a touch to her shoulder as he turns toward me. Her response is incomprehension turning to peevishness. Her mouth sets into a hard line.

My eyes lock on Landry, but in my peripheral vision, I see her notice me as the cause for Landry's abrupt departure. She scowls and spins on her heel, trudging back to the keg and the fire.

As Landry and I walk toward each other, space and sound telescope. I check my ragged breathing. There's something animal in the way he walks. There's a possession of his hips and legs in his blue jeans. He has long legs like me but he uses space differently when he moves. He commands breadth in his movement.

I smile and when we touch, he reaches out and runs his hand along my ear and hair. He starts to say something and then stops, pulling me to him with both hands and covering my mouth with his.

I feel his heart pounding and I hear mine in harmony.

We are on the same frequency. He feels safe because of his Leadville ties. I know his family. I know he understands mountain wisdom. I know he gets the craziness of this community, bitter and closed as it is.

But I didn't grow up with him. He's not someone who tortured me in eighth grade for my dorkiness. I didn't have American history and algebra with him. I didn't stand behind him in the cafeteria line or sit by him at pep rallies. He's familiar but not.

He holds me like he's never going to let go. The smell of him, the taste of his kisses, makes me light-headed. He blots out the sun, literally and figuratively. His warmth and his closeness are driving me insane.

Slowly the intensity of his desire subsides and I put my head on his shoulder, leaning into him. He caresses the hair that hangs to my waist.

He sighs and says, "Come with me."

He takes my hand and leads me into the forest. People wander through the trees, smoking dope, lying on the ground talking, drinking beer, moving to the music that blasts from someone's car stereo near the fire.

"Do you still remember December's foggy freeze," sings Ian Anderson. "When the ice that clings on to your beard is screaming agony?"

We cross a stream without getting wet, jumping from bank to bank onto the softening moss growth of early summer. We find a rock formation and climb it by shimmying up the cracks. I don't need help. I've been climbing rocks like this my whole life. I could scale it with my eyes closed but I like how solicitous Landry is, leading the way and reaching back to pull me to the top.

From the crest we survey the meadow, the campfire, and the increasing drunkenness of the crowd.

Jethro Tull's lyrics continue. "Aqualung, my friend, don't start away uneasy..."

Landry thumps his chest and lets loose with a Tarzan call. I laugh. It's the first time I've heard this open-air laugh, the clean, fresh sound of his love for being outside and not in dark, closed buildings.

"Doesn't get any better than this," Landry says, sucking in his breath when his eyes light on me, the fire in them dancing. His mouth is heavy with kisses I want.

Mischief sparkles in the brown depths of his glance. "What do you want from me?" he teases, like he's read my mind.

"Almost everything," I counter, kissing him slowly, lingering in the warmth of his mouth.

"Almost?" Landry asks, his lips brushing mine as he speaks.

"Almost," I confirm. I kiss him again and his mouth is delicious.

He moans low and deep in his chest and I feel my knees start to buckle. Being desired, being craved—is there anything more intoxicating?

Jethro Tull's lyrics carry on the spring breeze. "She signs no contract but she always plays the game."

He gently bites my lower lip, sucking my flesh between his teeth. I moan.

We break apart, laughing at our heat, the sweet sultriness of standing on a granite boulder, sliced with quartz, in the fading sun, kissing and touching and falling in love.

Chapter 19

We realize we've been on the rock for hours. The sun is slipping behind the mountain and the temperature is dropping. People have wandered past the rock formation, some of them seeing us, most of them not.

Landry watches the striations of light from the coming sunset. "You know you're beautiful, don't you?"

"No," I answer honestly.

"You are. Especially in this light." He turns to me.

I arch my back into the kiss that follows. It's languid and lingering and I can't get enough to fill the sudden emptiness inside me.

But the dropping temperatures win out.

"I'm cold," I say, shivering.

The bonfire sends up a shower of sparks. Someone is adding fuel and I can smell the pine pitch as it ignites.

"Glad to know I'm not the only one freezing my ass off," he laughs.

"Freezing to death is a regular occurrence at this altitude," I mumble.

Santana's Abraxas plays at the fire, reaching us across the chilling air.

"Come on, Black Magic Woman," he smiles, pulling me to my feet. He traces my jaw with his thumbs.

I throw my arms around him, squeezing tightly. I want him as close as I can get him. I know he's cold and I wrap my arms and one leg around him, trusting that his balance will keep us on the rock. I can feel his hands on my back.

"Thank you," he says finally.

We leave the rock reluctantly. We have danced and yodeled and talked on its surface for hours. The conversation, sprinkled between kisses, has ranged from music and wolverines to avalanches and backcountry skiing. We have talked mountain talk.

We are imprinted on the rock, and without a doubt, it will remember us forever, the couple who found, who climbed, who claimed and who fell a little more in love at its pinnacle.

"I like girls in hiking boots," he says, appreciating my rock skills as we descend.

"It's survival," I respond, knowing he understands that Leadville girls are a different breed than Pueblo girls. A different breed from all others.

We jump across the stream again, making a secure landing on the other side, and find our way back to the fire. We walk by three basketball players passed out under trees.

"They'll be okay?" questions Landry.

"Yeah, they'll sleep it off. Wake up when it drops below freezing tonight."

"You hope?"

"We depend on it," I confirm.

The fire blazes when we reach it, fueled up and shooting sparks to the sky.

"Ooooh, that does feel good," I say.

The radiating heat feels heavenly. I begin turning to get the warmth on all sides, like a rotisserie chicken.

Landry comes up behind me and presses himself into my back. His arms close around my shoulders and belly, covering me from behind so I can face the fire and watch the dancing flames. We are under a spell and Carlos Santana puts words to it.

"I need you so bad, Magic Woman, I can't leave you alone," whispers Landry as the song rolls into the next one, the guitar bleeding across the melodies.

The percussion kicks in with a haunting salsa beat. Landry spins me and takes me in his arms, pushing me into some quick dance steps. We move to the music, the intoxicating Latin beat, the guitar teasing at the edges.

I hear someone, it sounds like Steve, pick up the words, "Oye como va, mi ritmo," as Landry and I dance at the fire. Soon everyone is singing, grabbing for partners.

"Bueno pa' gosar mulata." It becomes a shout.

It's easy to dance with Landry. He moves with such assurance.

"Listen, how it goes, my rhythm." We have it, the rhythm. It's sexy and salty and I can smell Landry's skin and it's all so perfect.

Lyrics, entering the mind on the coattails of music, somehow bind themselves to the neurons in the brain so they are readily accessible under any state of consciousness. It's happening here. People sway and dance, from the alcohol and to the music, with only an occasional toppling.

It's the night before graduation and the stars are coming out, popping like a crown fire until the sky is ablaze.

The sound of Landry's voice is mesmerizing. He does not let go, and I think about spending eternity dancing in front of a fire with him singing in my ear and smelling like he does.

If I were a vampire, I would devour him. He wouldn't stand a chance.

Chapter 20

The song ends and Carlos launches into Incident at Neshabur, a fully-loaded instrumental.

The bonfire is an inferno leaping into the air when Landry pulls me to Clyde's Jeep. I start to shiver as the distance from the heat source increases.

When we reach the Jeep, Landry backs me into the driver's door and presses into me with the luscious heat of his body. He clasps my fingers with his and slowly lifts them behind my head, forcing my body to arc into his. His dark eyes are riveted on me. We are locked into each other.

Neither of us says a word. Our breathing becomes a series of slow, shallow, premeditated motions. He leans in and kisses me and it is warm and invites me for more. He's in no hurry and he kisses me as if he's going to kiss me all night.

I feel a moan rising inside me to match the hungry sound he makes when he touches me but I stifle it. I want this to last. I don't want my body to signal for more. Not yet.

His lips slide along my jaw to my neck and he pauses there. I hold infinitely still. I want this moment to last forever and he somehow senses it.

He releases my hands and enfolds me in his arms. I can feel our hearts beating, inches apart. There's a messaging that aligns with everything that is right in this moment.

I run my hands up his arms and settle my fingertips on his neck and the smooth, enticing skin there. His lips find my mouth again and his tongue feels like fire. My body shivers from the intensity of my response to him.

"Cold?" He breathes the question in my ear.

We both know I'm not cold. I'm on fire.

He pulls back and looks at me with desire in his eyes. I want him to want me like this. It ignites every cell in me. I'm flush with my own desire from head to toe and his nearness and focus on me are irresistible.

"Madelyn..." He says my name like a caress. "I want you."

But as soon as he says it, I know that I can't. I feel the fire drain out the bottoms of my feet like hot glass. I sag against the car.

"It's not safe," I say.

"I'll use protection," he says, not understanding.

"No, I mean something else." I touch his ear with my fingertip. I want to memorize him.

"What, Maddie?"

"I'm not ready."

"Ready for what? For sex?"

He can't begin to understand. I already know that. Whatever I say won't change it. "I haven't--I'm not ready--" I stumble across the words.

"You're a virgin?" he asks, looking deep into my eyes.

I nod my head. I know what's coming next. I've heard it before.

"I'll be gentle," he says.

"I know you will, but it's so much more than that."

"Tell me, Maddie."

"It's about how it's going to overwhelm my life. I already know that."

"No, Maddie. It's not such a big deal. It's the most natural thing in the world. You were born for this. It's why God made you this way." He tries to touch me but I avoid the contact.

How do I tell him about the knowing that I have? The comprehension that sex will shatter me, break me into a million pieces, leaving something unknown in its place?

"I'm afraid of the power of it," I begin but he's not listening now. He's clicking down the guy-wanting-to-get-laid agenda. And I've already heard every point on the list.

"I will still feel the same about you," he says.

He's off and running. How do I tell him about the complete disrespect that seems to arrive the second a girl loses her virginity? The awkwardness that I've observed, the snickers, the stupid meanness that burns my eyes like a hot poker every time I see it?

I can't decide whether to blink or not. Not getting a reaction, he proceeds to the next item.

"You don't know what this does to a guy. It's painful. You can't tease a guy like this."

Should I tell him how many times I've heard this? How many times do girls need to hear this before they become convinced of their obligation to provide relief? Maybe sixty times isn't enough, which is probably how many times I've listened to it.

"It's not a big deal, Maddie. You should do it and get it over with."

Check.

"I'm pretty sure I'm in falling in love with you, Maddie. But I need to know for certain."

Check.

That's when he notices my silence. And he does what no person has ever done before. He does something that takes my breath away.

He asks, "What do you mean—the power of it?"

My mouth drops open in surprise and I blink. My eyes burn.

"I--" Is he really going to listen to me?

"Tell me, Maddie," he affirms.

It could be a trick. Halfway through whatever it is I'm about to say, he could dump a boatload of humiliation on me.

I swallow. Do I dare? Am I capable of putting these thoughts into words? So far it's been a flash in my brain, a cold knowing in my gut. Are there words for this?

He's waiting. He's studying my face, looking intently into my eyes.

"It's something I know. Somehow," I tell him quietly.

"Go on," he says, listening hard because I'm speaking so softly.

"It's like I know. Even before I get there. To sex, I mean. I know that what they say, what we keep hearing, is all wrong."

I swallow. He doesn't interrupt me.

"They keep saying it's only sex but I know that it's not."

"But you've never had sex..." Landry says and I know he's trying to find my point.

How do I find words for this? How do I describe what I can't tell—that if it's anything at all, it must be everything?

I say, "I know. That's what makes this so hard. But it's more than what they tell us. It's more than anything they tell us."

How do I say that it must be a starlit communion, a defiance of boundaries, a yielding of the cosmos?

Landry asks softly, "What do you think sex is, Maddie?"

What do I think sex is? A breaking apart of everything definite—time, space, finite matter? A reconfiguration of the universe?

"I don't know but they're keeping something secret." I laugh. Where did I come up with "secret?" I sound like a conspiracy freak.

Landry is surprised by my laugh but he keeps listening.

I don't know what my body is capable of but I want to feel an ascension above the bounds of earth, beyond the realm of gravity and the five binding senses. I want it to create typhoons in

Thailand and ion storms on Saturn. I want astral fire to reach Andromeda.

I know it's time to make it lighter than it is. "Maybe I'm a Martian?"

"I doubt that," he says.

"You wouldn't really want to make love to a virgin Martian who wants to believe sex has the power to blow up solar systems, right?"

Landry pauses and the corners of his lips start to tug into a smile. "Maybe..." he teases.

I want the ethereal lift, the transcendence. I want him to die with me, just a little.

"It needs to be something more. I know I need to wait for whatever more is. Does that make any sense?" I ask.

"You sure know how to confuse a guy. You know that, don't you?" he asks but he's still smiling.

I need to trust that my body, in tune with his, will take us where it's breathless, glorious, other-worldly.

"It confuses me too, if that's any consolation. And I'm freezing," I finally admit, breaking into violent shivers.

Landry takes my hand solemnly and leads me back to the fire.

Chapter 21

The fire crackles as we warm ourselves. The Abraxas tape is ending. As Landry and I stare into the fire, an abrupt distance settles between us. The talk has added to and subtracted from our understanding of each other. We are absorbed in our own thoughts.

Lines from Meteor Shower repeat in my head. "Apparently, breaking out will take a whole bunch of will-power and a fair share of whistling in the dark. Because, after all, who knows what's out there?"

I look at Landry and he's watching the flames. He reaches for my hand, sensing my glance. I can tell he's thinking too. Soon he'll be in California and then, in all probability, in Vietnam. He's spoken for, in very real terms, for the next two years. I don't know what will happen after tonight. He may decide our discussion has left him too unsure of a physicality between us. He may be looking for a last hurrah, a fun jump before going into the service with no strings attached.

I want to believe he has some inkling of what I tried to tell him tonight. He could walk away and forget everything we've shared--dancing on the rock, the moonlight, the caresses, lying on the stage of the Opera House.

We are gauging the conversation in our heads. We are not talking. I'm tired to my bones. I have graduation in the morning, followed by a performance and another party in the woods.

If he's looking to get laid, I guess he can look elsewhere. I'm not interested unless it's everything that I sense it has the potential to be. I have settled all my life and I will not settle on this. I know I've set the bar very high but this is mine.

I'm too smart and too stubborn to believe sex means nothing. If it means nothing, then it's a waste of time.

"Why bother?" I ask myself and realize I have said it out loud.

Landry turns his gaze to me. "Pardon?"

I shrug and smile. We have talked and now it will be whatever it will be.

Clyde appears from the woods, laughing and joking with two girls, juniors who have appended themselves to the festivities. Graduation is currently the biggest show in town and they don't want to miss a minute.

Class distinctions fall away in a small school. We cheered each other on--in choir, band, shop projects, art, but never more than in sports. As athletes, we excelled.

At altitude, the blood gets thick. Oxygen molecules require extra hemoglobin and red blood cells to keep the body alive. It becomes a chronic condition that works to the benefit of athletes.

When Leadville's teams go down the mountain to compete, they have the extra edge for processing oxygen with amazing efficiency. Alternatively, when competitors come up the mountain, they're sucking wind, short of breath and disoriented. There's no compensating.

It's why we're small but powerful. We breathe thin air.

Chapter 22

"Well, I've got grace. And light. And gravity. But I can use all the luck you're inclined to wish me." I hear the lines from the play in my head.

It's getting late and I'm tired. And tired for me translates to cold. Landry is no longer covering my back so I'm once again rotating in front of the fire and assessing the distance between us.

I would like to slip away but that would be impossible. It's midnight, the witching hour when partiers start puking in their shoes. It's time for me to go but I can't think of a seamless way to escape.

Clyde yells across the bonfire, "Hey, Maddie. What's shakin,' girl?"

He comes around the fire with his arms spread, drunk and looking for a hug. I oblige. He's warm and safe and I listen to his distinct chuckle. He's breathing into my hair and I hope it will break open whatever needs to be broken open.

"Maddie, we are graduating tomorrow," he says into my hair. "And here I am--going to work in the mine. Just like my dad. Just like I said I would never do."

I know this and I know what it means to him. It means he didn't know what else to do. It means his fear got the best of him. It means he's scared to leave Leadville. It means he is settling. And tonight, settling seems like the worst thing in the world. It means the death of hope, the end of dreams. It crystallizes the possibility that the best time of our lives may be tonight.

I want so much for Clyde. He has so much potential. His music, his artwork, his portrait of Jimmy Hendrix and Janis Joplin, his incessant joking in English class, his prowess on the wrestling mat. I know his tenderness and his sensitivity. I don't know what becomes of all that at Stork Level in the darkness.

"Aw, cousin," Clyde says, reaching out to Landry to include him in our hug. "Cousin Landry, off to war."

As Landry joins our embrace, he puts his arm around me and squeezes tighter. He puts his face in my hair and I feel him soften. Whatever fight was in him dissolves and it's all right. For now, in this moment, it's all right. Clyde has not gone underground and Landry has not set foot in Vietnam. I will say lines in a monologue tomorrow that will define something for me and this town. I feel it in my bones.

The two juniors wiggle their way into the hug. They are small, delicious girls and their giggles penetrate my heart like soft bubbles. They don't know. Or maybe they do. They are a year away from this moment, standing at a bonfire, in a huddle of love and beer breath and resignation to whatever life is about to dish up.

Chapter 23

Graduation morning, the dawn is cold and clear. There has been some snow in the high mountains and a crisp wind rattles my window.

When I got in last night, no one was home. I slipped into my bedroom, locking the door against whatever insanity they might bring back with them. I turned out the light after staring at my graduation gown. It's purple, purple and gold being the school colors. The Panthers of Lake County High School.

I pulled the covers up to my neck, and lay awake for a while, watching the faint dance of the street light on my ceiling.

"Good night. Sleep tight. Sweet dreams," I murmured to myself, to Rusty, to Joel, to Landry.

After the hug, the group disbanded, loading into cars and going home. Landry hesitantly reached for my hand and kissed my fingers.

I thought about the last touch of his lips on me as I drowsily watched the ceiling. "Tomorrow," I thought, as I drifted off to sleep.

Whatever drama my parents brought home must have been fairly quiet because I slept through it.

When the sun comes up, cold and bright, I roll over and look at my graduation gown.

My thoughts are clear. Whatever happens today, no one is going to see me blink.

There's no way for me to know. The day will unfold however it's going to unfold. I will stare it down.

I take a shower and eat a bowl of Cheerios. I had hoped Rusty could get leave to come home for graduation but he's not here.

I will just do this.

I will just do this and open the door to whatever is waiting on the other side. I feel brittle, like my edges or my core has crystallized somehow overnight. I dreamed of Landry, the warmth of his hands and the depth of his eyes.

Suddenly I want to scream or smash something. I look around the house and realize no one would notice. Everything is wrecked, everything broken--the flotsam and jetsam of extended alcoholism. It takes everything, even the living room lamp.

"Let's go," I tell myself.

I throw my graduation gown and mortarboard in the Camaro, along with the bag holding the costume for the play.

I back out the driveway, the Camaro purring in the cold morning air, and head out past the cemetery. I take her up to ninety-five in the flats. I'm flying. I whoop once, pounding the steering wheel.

"Go, baby girl!" She's a magnificent creature, lean and vibrant. I have to believe the same about myself.

We slide together, one unit sealed together by fate, into the first curve, down-shifting, playing into the clutch. I hear the power train take her down and she smokes through the curve with the grace of a cat. I power out at the end of the curve and steer into the second line. It's a thing of beauty. I'm going so fast. The Camaro responds under my hands like she's reading my mind. Everything is in flow. My feet, my hands and the purr in my throat.

"Whoo hoo!" I yell exuberantly.

I realize I want everything. I want my life to be like this. I want it fast and exhilarating and heady and never for a moment dull. I suck in an excited breath as I slide through the third curve and over the hilly hump, catching air and landing like an angel.

This. This is what I want.

Chapter 24

When I hit the high school doors with my cap and gown in hand, Clyde is on me. He pulls me off to the side with a concerned look on his face. "What happened last night between you two?" he asks.

My heart drops.

"Why?" I ask, buying time.

"Landry's gone. Left in the middle of the night. Didn't seem mad or anything. Threw his stuff in a bag and said it was time to go." Clyde stares closely at my face, trying to read a reaction.

I don't give it to him. Never let them see you blink, I remind myself.

"I don't know," I manage, with a steely glance around to see if anyone can hear.

It's just us. All the emotions that well up in me will do me no good. Anger is the only negative emotion that doesn't paralyze. I reach for it and pull it on like an overcoat. "Maybe he got homesick."

Clyde gives me a strange and twisting look.

I turn and walk away. After five steps, I glance over my shoulder and call back to him, "How late am I?"

Clyde is already wearing his cap and gown.

"I--I don't know. I don't know," Clyde stammers.

"Okay. I'll see you in the gym," I call as I break into a run.

Running down the hall feels wonderful. I know because I've taken every opportunity. It's against the rules, it's loud and open, and this—this is my last chance to do it.

Parents are arriving, friends, siblings. I don't know if either of my parents will be here. It depends on what time they wake up and what condition they're in. They don't have my attention. They haven't had my attention for a long time.

Landry is gone. He has put miles between us.

I throw open the door to the locker room and head for the end of a row where I can gather my thoughts and nail down my emotions.

Everyone else is dressed, giggling, a little nervous, a lot self-conscious. Fortunately, no one tries to engage me in conversation.

I find an empty locker for my clothes. I untie my boots and kick out of them, pulling off my jeans and stripping my vest and shirt. And I suddenly feel the need to keep going.

I take off my bra and step out of my underwear, throwing everything in the locker. Naked except for my socks, I pull on the robe and zip it up. It's a cheap synthetic material and it's cold on my skin. It's just what I need. I don't want to feel anything on my body at the moment that isn't inferior and artificial.

"Yes, that's it," I say calmly to myself.

I sit down to lace my boots, and smile at the incongruity of my outfit. I have on hiking boots and a graduation robe and nothing else. No one will know about my nakedness but me. It feels like a victory.

I punch the air. "She's unassailable, folks! Undefeatable! Look at that form!" I whisper a commentary to my jabs.

In my boots, I'm invincible. I've forgotten to bring my flimsy dress shoes. The boots are perfect. The last thing I want to feel right now is vulnerable. My outfit is a statement and they will have to live with it. They will never know the extent of my statement. They will see a girl with long red hair in a purple robe and hiking boots. They will shake their heads, those who know me, and those who don't will look confused.

It's time to graduate. I put my cap on my head, check the mirror and find my place in line. The music starts for the processional and we march into the throbbing chaos of the gym.

Chapter 25

"I'm gone," I say out loud as I head up East Fifth Street, rocks flying beneath the tires.

The Camaro fishtails as she tries to find traction at the speeds I'm demanding of her. I need to get to the Diamond head frame and be there for a while.

All through the graduation ceremony, Clyde tried to catch my eye. I stared straight ahead at the stage, laughing appropriately, being serious appropriately. I listened to the speakers and applauded when I should.

I walked up on stage in my hiking boots and stared down the principal, who looked at my feet and then back at me with a disapproving glare. He and I have been crossways for years. He suspended me in December for singlehandedly breaking the dress code.

The code required female students to wear skirts or dresses no matter what. It didn't matter if it was twenty below zero with a wind chill of fifty below zero. It didn't matter if there were outside activities or theater projects that required climbing ladders or steps or working in the shop area. It didn't matter to him.

I'm sure he justified himself by saying it would make us ladies. It was apparent years ago to me that skirts are about sexual access. Of course. They make rape easy. They make women uniquely available and defenseless. It's a perpetuation of male entitlement and it has been that way for two thousand years.

It's why I'm naked under my robe. It's my rite of passage, not only from the dictates of my tiny little high school in a tiny, brutal town, but from the dictates of thousands of years of history in the hatred of women. I graduated clean and bare. And not a single person knew.

We threw our mortarboards in the air and I ducked out on Clyde. I ducked out on everyone. I grabbed my bag, threw my clothes into it and ran from the school wearing my hiking boots and cheap synthetic.

I did not look around during the speeches to see if my parents were there. I didn't wait to stick around afterwards. I don't want to know. I don't care. I need to get to the head frame.

"There," I breathe as I see it.

In shaft mining, a head frame holds the hoist equipment for lowering men into the mine and bringing up the ore. The Diamond head frame was constructed from wood timbers now darkened with age.

We pass it on our sled runs down Fifth Street every winter. We go at night so we can see headlights coming up. Flexible Flyers always. They run fifty miles an hour all the way down Fifth

Street into town. The secret is to aim for the darkest spot ahead because the trees reflect light. The darkest spot is probably the road. With any luck.

"Death wish?" I ask out loud. No, death is a side effect of living life at this speed at this altitude. "It's only fun if it can kill you."

I can tally a few broken backs and several head injuries among us but no deaths attributable to our running Flexible Flyers at fifty miles per hour.

"Maybe I should attach skis instead of runners." I like the idea. It would be even faster. Maybe I'll try it next winter.

When the snowplow clears the road down to dirt in places, the metal runners create friction, causing sparks to arc in a spray from the sled. It's a shower of light particles.

Fifth Street a five-mile run with dizzying dips and curves. It's sensorial--the sound of speed, the brace of cold, the pine smell, the taste of adrenalin on the tongue and a light show in the air.

I won't be here next winter.

Chapter 26

I slide the Camaro sideways to a stop when I reach the Diamond Mine and its old head frame.

I've played "In-a-Gadda-da-Vida" as I crossed town, the bass booming through the Camaro's speakers. The music coils inside my head, washing the pain over riffles of sand.

The first six minutes, the droning minor key riff took me from the high school parking lot to Harrison Avenue. The drum solo carried me to the head frame.

As I turn the key in the ignition, I leave it on auxiliary so the song can conquer the silence around me. I will want the silence soon but not right now. I want the ethereal organ solo and the tribal drums, the pounding bass and the angry voice over everything. The ether fits me.

I get out of the car and leave the door open to make sure the sound permeates the old mine like a cloak. I want my anger infused with this sound track.

He didn't get it. He didn't get what I told him. Or maybe he got it but he doesn't see the point. Or he thinks it's stupid. Or it scares him. Or all three.

I refuse the tears. I want to hold my anger close so I can get through the day. I have a performance and a party. I don't want this day relegated to a broken-hearted montage of emotional weakness.

"In the Garden of Eden, baby," I yell, picking up a handful of rocks and throwing them at the head frame.

The stones bounce off the timbers and fall into the shaft. I hear them, five seconds later, strike the bottom, several hundred feet down. I want to scream but I'm afraid it would come out as a keening. And I don't want to hear it.

"Don't you know that I'm loving you?" The coldness in Doug Ingle's voice soothes my jagged edges.

I stride around the Camaro, physically trying to enlarge the space of my torment. There's a scope to pain and if I can force it open, it will lose its compression.

"Oh, won't you come with me and take my hand?" The song interludes in cut time.

Seventeen minutes of Iron Butterfly's greatest and I'm physically delineating the boundaries of my agony. The burn zone is much bigger now, not as intense.

"Oh, won't you come with me and walk this land?" Lee Dorman rolls out the bass line.

The organ takes it up in a trill and the final six notes drop into silence as I reach in and shut down the tape.

I step away from the car and listen to the silence. I turn and look at Turquoise Lake in the distance, beyond the city of Leadville. My eyes sweep up to Mount Massive, and settle on the peaks called the Devil's Coffin and the Three Vampires. The sky is a crisp blue setting off the white snow-caps that stand stark and clean at the end of May.

It's not enough. As majestic and domineering as the mountains may be, they are not enough. I have things to do and it's too small here. At some point this summer I will load my belongings into the Camaro and go.

"Please take my hand," I whisper the last line of the song.

I wonder if my brother knew the Camaro would be my lifeline--my roots and my wings. It's his living bequest, his acknowledgement that he understands. He threw me a life preserver when he stepped out onto the seven seas.

He could have let me drown. His absence has felt like slow suffocation at times. He writes. He calls when he can. We don't say the important things. We never verbalize the depth. But what isn't spoken between us is so immediate that we might as well be talking in code. The exchange is subsonic.

"I wish you were here," I say to the sky.

We are able to reach across the distance in a way the government cannot control. It's a link that crosses all barriers. They cannot stop what we can do when either of us pauses and stretches across time and space to the other.

I hear him reply on the wind. He's the rustle in the leaves, the sigh on the breeze.

I close my eyes and listen.

I realize I'm hungry. I open the trunk and survey the cache of food I keep there. There's a change of clothes and a sleeping bag too. Because I never know.

I open a can of tuna and eat it with my fingers, watching a chipmunk jump across the floor joists of the old millhouse. It's eternally quiet.

With something in my stomach, I'm suddenly very tired. The emotional rampage has drained me.

I change into my civilian clothes, throwing the graduation gown into the back seat.

From the trunk, I retrieve the sleeping bag and lay it on the shady side of the car. Climbing in, I rest my head on my hands as I lie on my back and watch a few wisps of clouds move across the sky high overhead. The noon wind is picking up, bending the new grass, and that is the last sound I hear before I fall asleep.

Chapter 27

I wake up in the sleeping bag, rolled on my side. The shadows are longer and I look at my watch. It's four o'clock. Final rehearsal for the talent show starts in an hour.

I sit up, allowing the down bag to fall around my hips. Stretching, I listen for birdcalls but it's still too early. Even the robins have not arrived. That predicts at least one more big snowfall before summer finally gets a toehold on Leadville.

I crawl out of the bag, shake it out and return it to the trunk. I open a can of pears and dig for a spoon. They taste cold and refreshing. I know I need something else to eat before the performance. My stomach is growling but I feel sick from the emotional roller coaster of the day.

Landry is gone. In less than a week he will be in California, bunked in, under the calculating eye of a drill instructor. The Marines will have him. Standing there, at attention, he will think of me. He will have plenty of time to replay our last conversation. Maybe he will begin to understand. Maybe he will question. Maybe, deep in his gut, he will sense what I was saying.

I stand with the empty pear can in one hand and my spoon in the other. Dark clouds scuttle across Mount Elbert and Mount Massive. The temperature is starting to drop.

I stow the remains of my meal in the trunk and start the Camaro. The double pipes rumble and purr. I need to find that place—the place of rumble and purr. I have a performance to do and it will be the end of one thing and the beginning of another.

I feel strangely calm and rested after my nap on the ground. I know my hip is indented from small rocks even though I tried to brush aside what I could. It was obviously not a thorough job. I just wanted to lie down and make it all go away.

For the moment I seem to have succeeded.

Quietly I put the Camaro into first gear and roll away from the head frame. It's all downhill into town. I grab a brush from the console and drag it through my hair as I ease down Fifth Street in second gear. I check the rearview mirror. My eyes are hard but serene.

"I will survive this," I say into the mirror.

This is nothing compared to what else I have survived--when, as I child, I didn't know if I would be alive in the morning. Sometimes I wanted the fatal episode to happen so it would be over. I wouldn't have to live with the fear and the suspense anymore.

Once the boys discovered me, I found warmth, excitement and solace in their arms, touching until the frenzy set in, slowing it down, pushing away, making them pay it out, setting the pace. I loved the kisses. I savored each one like a fine jewel. Each kiss different, each boy his own style. Always believing it was the highest art form, I gave myself over to the kisses completely, abandoning all else. Kissing gloriously was my obsession.

But when Landry kissed me, it took me into deep space, into an unknown realm, a galaxy beyond this one.

I park behind the Opera House and swipe Chapstick on my lips. These are the lips that kissed Landry, as he pulled me into him, as he leaned me into the car, as he backed me into the wall.

I let myself in through a side door, slipping past the theater and up to the second floor. A few years ago a theater troupe from Northwestern University staged plays here. The men were housed in a rental house on Poplar Street; the women upstairs in the Opera House. A shower and bathroom was installed for them.

The shower is where I'm headed. I need to wash the unshed tears from my eyelashes, the anger from my skin, the howl from my throat. I strip off my clothes and wrangle the old plumbing.

The shower delivers me.

Chapter 28

When I make my way downstairs to the theater, it's lit up and noisy with laughter. My friends scamper up and down the aisles and under the stage lights. Their joy is infectious and I feel my heaviness lift. I laugh out loud as a cartwheel competition breaks out on stage. It might as well be a kindergarten graduation.

Not one to miss a cartwheel tournament, I jump onstage. I'm dressed in black from head to toe, ready for my performance but I cannot be deterred. I cross the stage in six spirited cartwheels, being careful not to wipe my hands on my shirt or pants when I'm done.

"Yea!" I cheer, adding to the celebration.

"Maddie," I hear my name and turn. Clyde catches me and holds me by both arms, looking with concern into my eyes.

"Maddie, where have you been?"

I shrug, "Fifth Street."

"Are you okay?"

I try to look nonchalant and unfazed. "Yeah, I'm fine."

"I've been worried about you." He pulls me in for a hug.

"I'm fine," I mumble from his chest.

"No, I'm asking you, are you okay?"

"Yeah, I'm fine. I told you, I'm fine. Didn't you see me ace the cartwheel competition?"

"Yeah, you did great but I'm still worried about you," he says again.

"Look, Clyde, Landry and I--it's all okay. We had a thing. He left. That's just the way this one went." I impulsively brush my lips across his cheek to seal the deal and wander off to watch the competition which now includes the hilarious efforts of the male classmates.

I spot Francie at the light board helping the tech, notes in hand. I can feel Clyde watching me but there's nothing more to say. Don't ever let them see you blink. Not even your friends.

The light tech runs through the sequencing at lightning speed, the cartwheel competition playing out under a kaleidoscope of changing colors and patterns.

There's something so logical about an acid-trip cartwheel contest in a hundred-year old opera house. It makes perfect sense. It's the only thing that does make sense.

Behind the scrim, a drummer plays a rhythm on drums and an electric guitar riffs. It's a feast of the senses. It all works and it's all mine to enjoy in this moment. It will never happen again.

Francie steps onstage and whistles, laughing at the exuberance around her. "All right, let's run this through. It won't take long if we do it at speed. I know there's a woodsie tonight."

A cheer goes up. There most definitely is a woodsie tonight.

She raises her hand for quiet. "The final order is on the sheet. Check with the stage manager if you have any questions. There are sure to be glitches but roll with it. You know everybody in the audience and everybody knows you. We'll give them the best show we can. It's all about the Class of 1971."

There's more applause and yelling. This is who we are and we happen to be really loud.

As everyone moves into position, I take my position onstage. I'm first. I set the tone. I set the bar for all the performances that come after me. I turn my back to the audience.

"Kill the house lights, Wally," Francie yells. "Bring down the stage lights."

Everything goes dark around me, an exhilarating sensation of expectation and promise.

"Quiet! Spot up from the back," Francie yells.

I hear the mechanical click of the old spotlight and I see my shadow on the backdrop.

"Anytime, Maddie," she says, softly this time. The theater is quiet.

And I start it off.

Chapter 29

Rehearsal is finished and the audience arrives. The theater fills with parents, siblings, neighbors, the mayor and city council.

I stumbled over one line, "I stripped whatever grace they had as I passed through." But I think I have it now.

I sat through the acts after my opening—"Mr. Bojangles" by Ronnie; the gymnastics exhibition; stand-up comedy by Terry; the cheerleaders doing a high-stepping routine to Golden Slumbers from the Abbey Road album; Clyde's band, The Grilled Cheese Incident, rocking the house with a cover of Sunshine of Your Love and an original piece called Strike Anywhere.

The quiet shuffling of the audience becomes a roar. They call out to friends, talking loudly, hitting flasks hidden beneath coats. Children shriek as they run around, jumping into the pit at the front of the stage, playing chase in the aisles. It's going to be a packed house.

Everyone is nervous, some a little, most a lot. Scattered in dressing rooms, backstage, and outside the stage door smoking cigarettes, their smiles are tight.

I sit on a stool by the light board, watching the audience through an opening in the side curtain.

When Clyde comes over, I reach for his hand and hold it. He's such a good friend. He knows what I'm feeling even though I would never admit it in a million years.

But he saw what was happening between Landry and me so when he smiles at me, I smile back.

"Hey, girl," he says quietly.

I don't want to think about Clyde going into the mine. He needs to be the singer in a rock-and-roll band, just like he's going to be tonight. He should have fans screaming at his feet, hanging on the meaning of his every lyric.

The buzz in the audience becomes an indistinguishable fracas. The stage manager signals Wally to flash the house lights. He points at me.

I lift Clyde's hand to my face and hold it to my cheek. I let go and take my place on stage.

I listen for the click as the house lights go off, followed by the dousing of the stage lights, as well as the overheads and offstage lights. The audience settles, murmuring softly.

The curtains open and the applause begins. There's an anticipation at this moment, always at this moment, in that second of time between the dying of the applause and the start of the magic.

The spotlight hits the back of my head and I see myself in halo. Dressed in black, my hair is the only source of color in the theater. I say my line with my back to the audience and I can sense them holding still.

I turn and look at them. They are not sure what I can see through the spotlight. I can feel their tensing. "Can she see me?" they wonder. I can see them and I cannot see them. From the stage, the audience is all and singular at the same time. It's a sea of faces but each face has a story.

I take my time with the lines. I feel my voice reaching the very back of the theatre, up into the balcony, like a net. I'm drawing them in. I'm forcing them to listen, to wait for me, letting it unfold at a pace I control.

I move across the stage. The lines roll out quicker now, in the heart of the play. I command the spotlight. It follows me everywhere I go. I talk to the audience without really connecting with them. There's intimacy and distance. When I laugh, they laugh. When I'm angry, they shrink back. When I challenge them, they look stunned.

And then I launch myself off the apron and land in the aisle.

It takes everyone by surprise, as it is supposed to. I've broken the invisible line between actor and audience. I'm too close to them and it sets up an entirely new dynamic.

I've felt my way intensely through the monologue. The emotions are right on the surface. I've accessed them in front of three hundred people and I'm raw and exposed. I'm feeling the pain of Landry again.

"I guess I'll be seeing you," I announce to the audience, saying the lines of the play. I muster my strength, in character, and begin whistling. I put my hands in my pockets and swagger up the aisle toward the back exit.

My whistle becomes more brave and confident and the audience turns to watch me. When I reach the back of the theater, I will go out the doors and my whistling will fade.

And then I see him. Landry is standing at the back of the theater.

Chapter 30

My whistle catches for a second but I grab for the character and find her. I resume, heading toward the doors where Landry stands, one leg crossed over the other, leaning against the wall.

As I pass Landry, I stay in character, being careful not to look at him. I know he's watching me because everyone is watching me. I whistle as I pass him and lightly skip down the staircase. I fade the sound to silence as I reach the lobby doors.

I pause to listen for the applause to start. It does. It starts, uncertain at first and grows louder, with stomping feet and approving shouts. They are blown away. It's a haunting and unique ending.

My heart pounds as it always does at the end of a performance.

I turn but not before I catch a glimpse of Landry coming through the theater doors at the top of the staircase.

I run.

Like a lunatic, I open the door to the street and take off, running hard down the sidewalk. I realize I'm heading south, which doesn't make sense, so when I hit Third Street, I turn uphill to the east. My head clears enough to realize I can turn into the alley and get to the Camaro. I glide around the corner, picking up speed. If I can make it to the Camaro, I'll be okay. She's there. She's red. She's safe.

I reach her, putting my hand on the door, and in a flash, I comprehend that the keys are in the Opera House.

Suddenly Landry is on me. He grabs my arms and turns me, pushing into me and forcing me back into the car. He kisses me, holding my face, hungry and beseeching.

We are both breathless. I can't believe he caught me. No one is faster than I am.

"You ran," he accuses me.

"So did you," I retaliate.

"I did. I'm sorry. I needed time to think."

That's when I start to hit him, landing frustrated punches on his chest.

He grabs my hands and holds them. "I understand what you were telling me."

I wrestle to free myself, crazed with frustration. "No, you don't. You can't. It's crazy."

He kisses me again. It's not an argument so much as a scream for help, for assurance, for both of us.

I find myself kissing him back. I feel my body responding. I'm angry at myself. I'm angry at him. I try to push him away but he holds me tighter. He kisses me until he feels the fight subside in me.

I hiss at him through my teeth. "I don't need you. I don't need anyone. Leave me alone. You don't know who I am. You don't want me. I'm in flight."

"We both know how to run."

I look at him and his flirty smile flicks at the corners of his mouth. His eyes are dark and dancing.

We are runners. Both of us. He has called it. It tickles under my ribs, thinking about the running we have both done to get here.

"Come here," he says, pulling me away from the car.

"No. It's not funny."

"No, it's definitely not funny," he says, setting me more evenly on my feet so I'm not pinned against the metal but still in his grasp.

"It's really serious," I say with a whine, feeling a grin pulling at my lips.

"I know," he says, his eyes flashing with unexpressed humor.

"It's incredibly serious. It's more serious than anything in the world. It's more serious than anything in the galaxy."

We are laughing. My heart is doing flip-flops in my chest. It's all mixed up in pain and laughter and giddiness and relief and exhaustion.

Landry strokes my face, touching my hair. The tears in my eyes are from the laughter. I'd like to believe that.

"It's okay," he says. "I needed some time. I understand what you were saying. It was a lot to take in at first. It's not the way I ever thought about it. You just go down that road. That road they tell you about."

I'm freezing, standing in the night air with no coat. "Come here." I need to move this conversation someplace warmer. Closer to my keys.

"What?" he says, surprised.

"Come with me. I'm freezing." I take his hand and lead him through the side door of the Opera House and up the stairs to the room where I where I showered. Where I left my keys.

"Just be quiet," I warn him. "I'm not supposed to be up here."

"Okay. Quiet," he whispers.

He gasps when I open the door and flip on a small light. The grand arched windows showcase the Presidential Range behind the glass. They are the white-tipped mountains that frame my life, clearly illuminated even though the moon is only a slice, a waxing crescent.

The high ceiling is ornate tin plates, complimented with hanging chandeliers. The original wallpaper has faded to a buffed gold and red. The floor is worn to an elegant patina.

"Wow," he says.

"Yeah, can you imagine what it once was?" I look around for a place to sit, some place safe and sure.

"This is cool," he adds, wandering to the windows and looking out across the lights of Leadville to the towering Rocky Mountains.

We stand, our shoulders touching. It's warm, the heat from the theater rising through the floor and walls. We can hear Ronnie performing Mr. Bojangles, the lyrics floating up with the heat.

"He spoke with tears of fifteen years how his dog and him, he traveled about," the voice sings.

Slowly Landry turns from the view to me. I look at his face, the dark, smooth skin and the eyelashes that frame the luxuriousness of his brown eyes.

He kisses me softly. I close my eyes and feel his lips.

The song finds its way into the room. "His dog up and died, he up and died, after twenty years he still grieves."

"I made it to Pueblo about four o'clock in the morning but I kept driving out to the plains. I stopped and watched the sun come up and then I went back to my Mom's house and slept."

I don't know why he's telling me this. I'm dazed by his closeness, by the fact that he's here at all.

There's nothing for me to say. I lean into him, into what he's telling me.

"You said it needs to be something more," he says, tracing his lips across my ear. "I didn't know what you meant. All I've ever heard is scoring and hitting it and screwing. And that's been fun, don't get me wrong."

I have to laugh. I take his hand and pull him to sit on a bed close to the windows.

"Mister Bojangles, dance..." comes the end of the song as the applause breaks out.

Landry turns to me, lying back on the blanket roll he has claimed. His eyes are blazing with intensity and my heart pounds in response.

"I want to know more. Tell me. Please," he says.

His words create pools of desire in my belly.

"Landry, I don't really know what I'm talking about. I've never had sex. I've avoided it because of the emotional messiness it brings."

"Go on," he says, reaching out and tracing my fingers with his.

I make my attempt at explaining, at putting into words what I know but don't know. "That it feels like a sneeze. A physical release. And then everyone goes to sleep."

He laughs. "It feels pretty damn good, Maddie."

"I know it sounds crazy but I want it to be more than that."

He pauses and I know he's analyzing my words. "Do you think it's technique or what?"

"I think it's a feeling. I think it's something total, something that connects us with the stars."

We both laugh again. "This is the part about blowing up solar systems," he teases.

I smile. We both know it is. He raises my hand to his lips. I shudder at the touch of his mouth.

"Pretty trippy, huh?" I concede.

"So what's the "more" part of it, Maddie?" he asks. "Love?"

I shake my head. "Word's too nebulous." For me, the concept of love is carelessly obscure.

"You want to wait until marriage?"

I hear the words come out of my mouth. "I don't want to wait another second."

He's as surprised as I am. We blink at each other.

I blush. I can't help it. "Where did that come from?" I try to make a joke of it but his eyes hypnotize me.

"Do you know how much I want you?" he asks, rising on his haunches to move his body across the bed to me.

"No," I say quietly.

"I would move heaven and earth to be with you," he whispers huskily.

I feel a drawing-down inside of me, but instead of continuing down, it starts to move outward and up, through my belly and into my lungs. It feels lighter and less dense than I've ever felt it before.

He leans into me, supporting himself on his arms, and he kisses me with slow desire. Every cell in my body wakes up and a hunger laces through my veins like liquid nitrogen.

His kisses are lazy and endless. The warmth of his mouth tantalizes mine, the flesh of his lips seeking and inviting.

"I want to take my time with you," he says softly.

"I don't know the way."

He smiles sweetly. "I know."

His kisses become more urgent, asking for more desire. I give it, wrapping my arms around his shoulders and pulling him closer.

He pushes the blanket roll onto the floor, easing me back onto the bed. He lowers his weight onto me, heavy and sensual. The feel of his body pressing against the length of me makes me gasp and moan. It's an exquisite sensation—feeling his chest, his hips, his legs against mine.

There's a heat brewing in my belly, reaching a boiling point. It radiates from deep inside me.

"You're all I can think about," he says, moving his scorching lips to my neck, tracing with the tip of his tongue.

I'm swimming in desire, my body answering his call. I have to feel his skin. I pull his shirttail out of his waistband and slide my hands up his back.

His body is toned and smooth and I feel him shudder from my touch.

His hands find my hair and he grabs handfuls of it, wrapping it in his fingers and pulling my head back as his kisses intensify.

I close my eyes and draw in a feverish breath.

"I've never wanted anyone like this," he says, searing me with his words.

I can feel his want in the heat of his body, in the way his tongue plays on mine. I wrap my legs around his and pull his hips into me. I feel the hardness below his belt. What I've always avoided before, I want with abandon now.

He tugs my turtleneck, loosening it from the black pants. Putting one hand under my shoulder blades, he lifts me off the bed and pulls the shirt off with the other hand.

I raise my arms as he slides the fabric over my head. The cool air feels splendid on my steaming skin.

His fingers release the hook on my bra as he lowers me onto the bed. I reach for his hair, dark and thick. His mouth descends on my collarbone. He traces the structure of it with his chin.

"You are luscious," he says, his lips finding the swell of my breasts at the edge of my bra.

I tremble as he slowly slides the bra away, over my shoulders and arms. I feel the warmth of his hands on the delicate flesh.

I breathe out. My words are gone. I'm aware of every movement, of every sensation.

His lips find one nipple and then the other, playing a temptation game. His hand gently squeezes the flesh, the palm massaging.

My breasts swell in response and the nipples harden. A delicious shot of electricity goes all the way to my groin.

I'm writhing and I know it but I can't stop. I don't want to stop. I'm dancing under his touch, slowly, rhythmically. My hips move in time to the throbbing I feel between my legs.

Pulling himself up onto his haunches, his sultry mouth finds my belly. His hands, sure and confident, follow my ribs to my hips. He traces the waistline of the pants.

I can feel his fingers on my skin as he checks for a zipper or buttons. But what I'm wearing is a dance costume, elastic and free to move in. It was perfect for the play. And now, as I lift my hips, it's perfect for him to slide over my hips and legs, stripping my panties, socks and ballet slippers as he goes.

I am naked. I can't open my eyes. I wait for his reaction and I hear him moan. He likes what he sees. I am long and lanky and the moan tells me everything I need to know.

"Good God," he says and I feel my body ease out of its apprehension.

"Touch me," I hear myself say. "Touch me."

And he does. He puts his hands on me, tracing my legs, caressing my hips, the curves of my back, the roundness of my bottom.

The desire in me burns through my inhibition and I sit up, reaching for his shirt and pulling it over his head. His chest is the color of milk chocolate and I put my hands on him, running my fingers over his muscularity, the firmness of his flesh.

He looks down at me, watching me touch him. His eyes are dark with wanton sensuality and I know how he feels. There's a luxuriousness to this, knowing we have all night, here, in the

Opera House, the stars and gleaming mountains waiting patiently.

But patient does not describe me. I'm hungry for him. Lust boils in my veins. I don't know the way but I do. I'm running on instinct, dropping into another level of being—one where there are no words, no conscious thoughts.

His mouth, full of desire and longing, makes me claw the mattress beneath me. Everything in me throbs to the beat of my heart.

I find his belt buckle and fumble with it. He concentrates on the kiss, slow, deep and forever. I'm burning alive with frustration as my fingers try to undo the buckle.

Landry saves me, laughing softly and standing slowly, trailing his fingers over me, to unbuckle his belt and kick out of his boots. He pushes his jeans to the floor and steps out of them.

I want to run my eyes over his body but his eyes lock into mine and I'm hypnotized. I know he's beautiful. I know he's built like a Roman god. My peripheral vision gives me that much.

"Maddie," he says, covering my body with his.

I wrap my arms around him. I want as much contact with his heat as I can get. I twine my legs around and through his. I run my fingers through his hair, clutching the dark thickness of it. My fingers find his neck, the heft of his shoulders, the narrow waist, the silkiness of his hips. I want to memorize him.

I can't get close enough to him. He's beautiful and I'm in love with him but I will never say it first and I don't care because I know it and it's what is giving me this cascade of feeling in my body, my body, my body.

He uses his knees to spread my legs apart. I'm so wet my thighs are slick. I close my eyes and raise my arms over my head. I reach and exhale, arching my back.

"Yes," I sigh and I let go, relaxing into the feel of him, hard and hot.

He's gentle. He moves into me slowly, a little bit and then a little bit more.

It burns. I feel a moment of panic. He stills, watching me closely.

"Okay?" he asks.

I nod bravely but I'm scared and he knows it.

Without moving any further into me, he kisses me again. His kiss has so much love that I lose myself in the taste of his mouth. His tongue finds mine and his lips are bewitching me. Has a kiss ever felt like this?

He kisses me again and again, each time with more intensity, with more fire. I find myself touching his face, sliding my fingers through his hair, pulling him closer, wanting him.

And then he moves again. And it burns but I don't care. I want his mouth. I want his skin. I want the weight of his body. I want his hands on me. I want him inside me. He has turned me into a blazing torch and I move against him. He slides all the way into me and the fullness of it is overwhelming.

I hear him catch his breath, raggedly, and I know he is overwhelmed too. We don't breathe. It's excruciatingly powerful. We hold on to each other tightly as the world threatens to come apart.

He moves again, easing back. My senses are in chaos. The boundaries between taste and smell and sound break down.

He eases in and out of me, feeling me, exploring me. "Oh, my God," I hear him breathe.

The slowness of what he is doing melts my core. Long frozen, long buried, I feel it soften and unwind. There's a slow uncoiling in me, in the deepest part of me.

My sensitivity is heightened in surrealistic ways.

He moves, with seamless fluidity and I'm half crazed with the intensity of what I'm experiencing.

"I can feel everything," I hear myself but it echoes like I'm light years away.

He moans and the depth of the sound triggers a sensation like the brush of a butterfly wing deep inside me.

I feel him swell inside me and he holds me tighter, searching for my lips and finding them.

I can feel all of him and every move he makes adds a delirious dimension to the quivering that intensifies in my darkest place.

He moves and then pauses to clench his jaw. His eyes are squeezed tight. I hear the word Rapture as if someone has spoken it in my ear.

And slowly he loses control, his movements becoming sweeping pulsations. He groans and I feel the length and breadth of him inside me and it's the most intense feeling I've ever experienced.

The flash comes up in me like sheet lightning and I hear the roll of thunder like a spring storm. I gasp as the heavens open up and the stars rain down on us and a solar wind takes the world apart.

And the sky falls to earth in a meteor shower.

The End

METEOR SHOWER

A One-Act Play by Carol Bellhouse

Dedicated to Tammy Stepisnik

Copyright 2013 Carol Bellhouse

Feel free to perform this play without charge.
Let me know how it goes.
CarolBellhouse@gmail.com

METEOR SHOWER

By Carol Bellhouse

A monologue for a single female actor, the stage is set simply, with two spotlights. The actor is dressed in black. Her back is to the audience.

TAMMY
When I was born, the sky fell to earth in a meteor shower.

She turns to the audience and observes coolly, judging.

TAMMY
It's not enough just to be born, you know. Not even in a meteor shower.

She pauses and looks offstage.

TAMMY
Since it ends in the blink of an eye, in one final exhale.

She examines the perimeters of the stage, feeling the invisible walls with her hands.

TAMMY
Once born, I must identify the confines of this life. And understand what I can survive.

She checks out one side wall and moves to the back wall, speaking over her shoulder.

TAMMY
My parents divorced after I was born, a stormy, noisy matter that played out never far from my crib. My confines of safety. I watched the violence as wallpaper in motion.

She feels along the last wall, bringing her back to stage front.

TAMMY
They were rough people. What came into me was the best of both, leaving them with nothing. Drained out, they became pumice stone—empty, jagged, blasted.

She stops and smiles as she again faces the audience.

TAMMY
Which makes me what – pumiceous?

She ponders it.

TAMMY
Polished. Smooth.

She nods in satisfaction at the change in adjectives.

> TAMMY
> That sounds better. Anyway, they were there but not there. They flailed, trying to find what I had taken from them at birth – some sense of it all, some grace.

She muses.

> TAMMY
> Grace.

She takes the first ballet position as she recites the definitions of the word.

> TAMMY
> Charm, elegance, especially of a delicate, refined, or unlabored kind.

She assumes the second ballet position.

> TAMMY
> A sense of what is right and proper.

She takes the third ballet position.

> TAMMY
> Decency and thoughtfulness toward others.

She takes the fourth ballet position.

                    TAMMY
          Mercy and good will.

She moves into the fifth ballet position.

                    TAMMY
          Unconstrained and undeserved favor.
Tammy pirouettes in the spotlights.

                    TAMMY
          Divine love.

She ends her dictionary recitation.

                    TAMMY
          I stripped whatever grace they had as
          I passed through. I took it all. Not
          purposely, you understand. That's just
          the way it happened.

          Separately now, they skitter through
          their lives, like fishing lure over
          water…from place to place, job to job,
          lover to lover. In the spirit of the
          sixties but lacking the passion. Doing
          it by rote. By habit.

She moves toward a stage wall but
becomes acutely aware of its presence and
backs away. She is trapped on stage.

TAMMY

They're weary. I can see it in their
eyes and in the softness around their
mouths. Life has disappointed them.

Tammy casually runs her fingers through
her hair as the spotlight comes up full,
making her radiant.

TAMMY

I was told–not by my parents, of
course, who were bashing it out in the
kitchen–that the light of the meteors
was born into me that night.

And that is my second gift. The light.
Illumination. That you can actually
see. Look hard. Squint your eyes–like
this–if you have to. Do you see the
meteor inside me?

Born under falling stars, I can burn
through space and time. I have and
will. The more friction, the brighter the
burn.

This is what you don't understand—A
meteor is actually a block of ice.
It's really very simple. When you get
too close to a meteor, you don't
scorch. You freeze.

Tammy laughs in a mixture of sweet innocence and gleeful malice. She is both younger and far older than her years. The implications and contradictions of what she is saying weighs in her voice.

> TAMMY
> So there's grace... and light. The third element—

She gestures around the stage.

> TAMMY
> My confines. Should I take my confines seriously? Should I obey their restrictions? The laws of nature? The laws of gravity? Or should I step across this wall? Become more than I am be expected to be? Outside my confines, how can I survive? What can I survive? And who will help me?

She narrows her eyes and challenges the audience.

> TAMMY
> If I reach out to you, will you help me escape this?

She raises her hands slowly to encompass her stage-prison. Even slower, she extends her arms to the audience, holding out her hands for help.

TAMMY
(slowly)
And what will you want from me in
return? What's your price? What kind
of person are you?

She asks earnestly—

TAMMY
Will you help make both of us better
people? Is your offer made in the
interest of brotherly love? Of the
kinship of sisters? Of uplifting
humankind?

She narrows her eyes slowly and continues
to the next level—

TAMMY
Or will you ask me to admire and
praise you as a mentor, a teacher, a
guide?

Her tone becomes hard:

TAMMY
Will you expect me to rub your back?
Your feet?
(pause)
Your thighs?

Tammy runs her hands down her stomach and thighs suggestively, while staring down the audience. She holds the stare until the audience shifts uncomfortably.

She laughs, throwing back her head and breaking the tension.

TAMMY
Isn't it all so…predictable?

Tammy tips her head and turns away from the audience. When she turns back, she speaks again—

TAMMY
What I want is this--to live my life with dignity and elegance. To be happy whether I'm alone or in family. To have the four basic necessities of life: food, shelter, clothing and a hot tub.

She smiles comfortably and shrugs.

TAMMY
If water is the essence of life, then so be it. I'll stay immersed up to my neck. One-o-four, here I come.

She stretches and cups her hands behind her head, luxuriating in an imaginary Jacuzzi.

TAMMY

When I was little, I loved to climb trees. The higher, the better. Way up in the sky, I never wanted to come down. To what? Swaying in the wind, so far above the ground, I was invisible.

The sun on my face. The tree whispering her lullaby all day long. One clear night, not long ago, I climbed a tree… all the way to the top. Scratched my elbow. Tore my jeans. There was no moon. It was well past midnight.

I stood on the highest branch and called out to the sky. I threw my head back and howled, "Show me! Show me!"

And when I opened my eyes, it came from the north and sailed clear across the sky.

She motions as she tells the story.

TAMMY

Then two, three, in short flares. And a fourth on the horizon. And when the fifth started its arc, I let go.

She pauses.

                    TAMMY
                   (slowly)
Falling to earth.
Like the stars.
Birthright.
I fell in slow motion, listening to my
breath. It felt weightless, like drifting in
a tide. Spinning, turning slowly. I
wondered if I'd hear my last breath.
When it flows out and stops forever.

Another pause. Tammy arches her
eyebrow.

                    TAMMY
But... it's not enough just to die, you
know. Not even in a meteor shower.

With humor, she explains:

                    TAMMY
A branch caught me by the back of
the belt. Almost snapped my neck.
Took me 45 minutes to get down. A
mosquito kept stinging me, buzzing
around my face as I dangled there.
Trying to crawl in my ear and land in
my eye.

Now I know what it's like to hang on a
branch, flailing, with something biting
you. And it'll be a long time before I
do it again.

She walks upstage, enjoying the funny
sensibility of it.

TAMMY
I now acknowledge the presence of
three forces in my life: Grace, light,
and gravity.

Tammy looks hard at the prison of her
stage and makes a life decision.

TAMMY
In my life, I will choose not to take my
confines seriously. I will elect not to
obey their restrictions…with the
exception of gravity, of course.

She moves to stage front.

TAMMY
I will become more than I am
expected to be. I will not allow my
confines to be my limitation.

She makes a move toward the audience
and backs away in fear as she reaches the
threshold.

She laughs at herself.

>   TAMMY
> Apparently, breaking out will take a
> whole bunch of will-power and a fair
> share of whistling in the dark.
> Because, after all, who knows what's
> out there?

For a moment, the fear in her is evident and
she asks herself the hardest question.

>   TAMMY
> Shouldn't my "childhood," my
> "background," my "family roots"
> dictate all that is to follow?

She pauses and thinks hard.

>   TAMMY
> No.

With tremendous determination, she takes
a deep breath and launches herself out of
her stage-prison, landing lightly and slightly
dazed in the audience. She looks around
and checks herself to make sure she's still
in one piece.

>   TAMMY
> Wow.

She takes a deep breath to build up her
courage.

                    TAMMY
          Well. I've got grace. And light. And
          gravity. But I can use all the luck
          you're inclined to wish me.

She takes another deep breath.

                    TAMMY
          I guess I'll be seeing you.

She assumes the posture of a little boy
walking home frightened in the night. She
starts to whistle against the dark, sputtering
dryly at first but gaining in confidence as
she moves up the aisle.

By the time she reaches the back, her
whistle is brave and nothing has grabbed
her yet, so it must be working. She exits
expectantly, whistling her tune.

The End

About the Author:

Carol Bellhouse is an attorney, writer and photographer living in Leadville, Colorado. At 10,100 feet, life has never been boring. She travels to great places like New Zealand, Hawaii and the catacombs underlying Paris.

An award-winning playwright and screenwriter, *Fire Drifter 1: Meteor Shower* is her first novel. She has previously published two poetry books: *Loving the Cowboy* and *Never More Beautiful*.

Current projects include a biography of Darwin Lamb of the Las Vegas dynasty, a young adult series titled *Mining Stardust,* and Madelyn Tremaine's continuing adventures in *Fire Drifter 2*.

Website: www.CarolBellhouse.com

Scripts by Carol Bellhouse:

Meteor Shower
Edge
Guido, My Guardian Angel
Cross Roads
Crystal Carnival
Kill for You
Anorexic Psycho Killers of Leadville
Ice
Ghosts in the Graveyard
The Vessel
Dancing in the Sand
Stacy
Missing Pieces
Strawberries, Brooms and Pelicans
Unfinished Conversation
Marilyn
Vegas Knights

Acknowledgements:

A boatload of thanks to my daughter Whitney and son Mike for being the Zen Masters in my life; Dawn Beck for doing massive amounts of heavy lifting; Tammy Stepisnik, Shelly Evans, Allison Finney Maruska, Jenny Po Loyd, Ed Finley, David Long, Pamela Wang, Belle Heyborne Shober, Kim Wallach and Christine Cortney for feedback and editing; and Tina Erickson Westphal for endless transcription.

Made in the USA
Charleston, SC
17 November 2013